S0-BIP-518

Where to now, Blue?

Where to now, Blue?

by
ADRIEN STOUTENBURG

Four Winds Press   New York

For Michelle Diane Baker

Library of Congress Cataloging in Publication Data
Stoutenburg, Adrien.
Where to now, Blue?
SUMMARY: Twelve-year-old Blueberry's attempt to run away from her poor home in rural Minnesota with a six-year-old tagalong from the orphanage ends in frustration, but as a result Blueberry becomes more sure of her plans for the future.
[1. Runaways—Fiction. 2. Poverty—Fiction]
I. Title.
PZ7.S8884Wh [Fic] 78–4336
ISBN 0–590–07518–7

Frontispiece by Donna Diamond

Published by Four Winds Press
A division of Scholastic Magazines, Inc., New York, N.Y.

Printed in the United States of America
Library of Congress Catalog Card Number: 78–4336
5 4 3 2 1 82 81 80 79 78

Contents

The Special Morning

THE HOUSE UNDER THE SCRUBBY PINES had a crippled look; a house that almost seemed to need crutches. In places, wind had torn the black tar paper tacked to the building's sides so that when the breeze gusted up from the Chicksaw River one loose strip tap-tapped over and over.

The tapping was the first thing Blueberry heard when she opened her eyes. It was as familiar as the squawk of the skinny chickens in the yard or the deep, sad baying of the Iversons' mongrel hound at the edge of town. Far off, a jet plane made a ripping noise through the sky; then silence as if the sky had closed right over the rip.

She rubbed her eyes, trying to shake off the dream of a handsome, large house where a tall man in an elegant suit embraced her, saying, "I've been waiting for you, my dear."

She started up, suddenly remembering where she was. This was The Day! There it was, circled on the Farmer's Bank calendar above her bed. May twelve. She had chosen the twelfth because it was her lucky number and because she herself was twelve. For one delicious moment, she lay still, pondering, then sprang up so quickly the bed almost collapsed.

Something crashed from the orange-crate bedstand. Smith the cat leaped from the foot of her bed.

"Damnation!" Blueberry exclaimed. Then "Damn" again. She wanted to stop swearing now that she was starting out on a new life! She picked the framed photograph up from the floor and inspected it anxiously. "No more cracked than it always was," she whispered to Smith. An earlier crack cut straight across Tad's chin. She swallowed against a tightness in her throat. "Only hope we didn't wake up the whole blasted house."

Smith said nothing. He sat sulking, miffed at having been awakened so rudely.

Ma and Pa still seemed to be asleep. Blue dusted Tad's photograph with the tail of the old shirt she wore as a nightdress, then laid it beside the gear she had hidden under her bed. Ma didn't usually bother to come into the room, and about the only time Pa ever had was when he sneaked in to find the perfume.

"No kid of mine," he declared, "—even if she ain't my real kid—is gonna go around stinkin' like a cheap floozy!"

She would never forgive Pa for what he had done. Blueberry brooded as she pulled on her jeans. Well, he wouldn't have a chance to go around mocking, "Blueberry, Blueberry, mean and contrary," any longer. Better than being dumb and shiftless like him! Anyhow, her real name was Linda. Hardly anybody called her that; her eyes were exactly the color of blueberries, everybody said. Could be worse, she often thought, like being named after a fish or a frog.

Smith scratched at the bedroom door. Blueberry opened it, commanding softly, "You stick around close now. We're shoving off the minute I get everything stowed on the boat. Remember, or I'll turn you inside out!" She gave his high-riding tail an affectionate tweak. She couldn't go anywhere, even on this glorious journey, without dear Smith. Or without Hunch either. She looked toward the parrot in his cage, then tensed.

There was the clatter of a stove lid on the wood-burning range in the kitchen, the rasp of a grate opening. Pa was up! Early. His voice tore the silence. "Get outta here, you sneakin' tom-devil!"

She ran out of the narrow bedroom and into the kitchen. "You leave Smith alone!" She grabbed Smith up, consoling, "Here, honey—did he hurt you?"

Pa grinned, showing brown stumps of teeth. "He was after the sardine can settin' out here where somebody left it. I gave him a good taste of boot leather like he deserves."

"He deserves something decent to eat once in a while. Animals have rights, too!"

Pa grunted, feeding corncobs into the fire. He aimed his mouth toward the woodbox, missed, and a wet brown blob of tobacco steamed and sizzled on top of the stove.

Blue shuddered. She let Smith outside. "You're up kind of early, aren't you, Pa?"

"Gotta important job at the gas station this mornin'. Constable Bemis wants me to grease up his car. You kin get to work now, too—hustle out that syrup in the cupboard and lay the table."

Some constable, Blueberry thought, and some town! Chicksaw Landing wasn't even on most maps. She followed Pa's orders mechanically. Best to be on her good behavior this morning of all mornings. The sun, she saw, was rising now above the cottony mists on the Chicksaw River, ready to polish things up for a sparkler of a day. Oh, it was going to be gorgeous! Everything! Only, she had to be very careful. There were lots of creeping little dangers. And Ma, once she managed to come awake, had a nose for anything wrong.

But if everything went well—and it *had* to—she and the *Victory* would soon be on their way down river. First, she had to try to steal some extra food to add to what she had already smuggled on board.

Pa fried some cold mush, now and then wiping the back of his hand against the snoose juice leaking from one corner of his mouth. "Tell your ma to git up and start the coffee, like a workin' man's wife should."

"Tell her yourself!" She couldn't stand the sight of him anymore—or his awful grease rack smell.

She hurried out before he could give her a "taste of boot leather," and went down the weedy path to the privy. She wasn't afraid of Pa. Heron-legged though he was, he couldn't run fast for long without coughing and getting out of breath. The couple of times he had caught her he didn't whip her too hard if only because he was too lazy or maybe too weak. Ma was different. One good quick slap from her and you could feel it sting for a long while.

Blueberry sat in the outhouse, looking out through the half-open door. The grass, what little there was of it, began to glitter in the sunlight, still keeping a bit of dew on its thin blades. The grass tried but it didn't have a chance against the burdock and dandelions. She and Tad had worked to help it along, pulling bushels of weeds, but the grass would have to look after itself now.

There were flies buzzing over chicken dirt, and two house wrens flitting around each other. Courting, she guessed, but there was no time to watch, pretty though they were.

She could not help humming as she went back to the house, so impatient to get started in the *Victory* that her heart seemed to throb faster than the wrens' quick wings.

Pa was making his own coffee. Ma seldom got up early, as Pa well knew in spite of his big talk about what a wife should or should not do. Ma just listened and let it go out both ears, then did as she pleased.

Blue went past Pa to the pantry to scrape up some kind of food for herself. She was too excited to be hungry but it was smart to try to eat as much as she could; there was a limit to how much she could stow on the boat. She wasn't due at school until later because of the split sessions. It seemed to her sometimes that the best thing Chicksaw Landing people did was produce kids to crowd the little schoolhouse.

From the corner of her eye, she saw Pa finish his own breakfast, then slouch out. Quickly, she finished what he had left of the fried mush, and forced herself to swallow some dry cereal with milk, then swabbed the table and hurried back to her room. Now, at last, she could make her first trip of the day down to the river. She bundled various articles in her arms, then picked up Hunch in his cage.

He gave a startled squawk before calling out hoarsely, "Onward and upward!"

"Sh-h-h!" she appealed. "That's for later." She listened; the room where Ma slept remained silent.

Once outside and on her way along the path to the river that angled out of sight below the house, she wished she dared to give a joyous shout of her own. For, oh, the morning was so full of promise. There at the river's quiet edge the *Victory* was waiting at anchor. How beautiful it looked! It was a pride and a glory, that ship, built by Tad's own hands, with her help. Re-built, actually, because it had been abandoned by its former owner. They had caulked, patched, and remodeled for two whole summers, using whatever scraps of material they could find or bargain for.

"You take good care of that boat," Tad had said before he left. "Someday we'll sail her all the way to the Mississippi and down to New Orleans."

He hadn't said where he was going that night, and probably didn't even know. He had mentioned something about hitchhiking out west, following the crops, or heading up to Alaska, or signing on a ship to see the world. Mostly, he kept repeating, "I have to get away, Blue—there's nothing for me here. The worst thing is leaving you. That's what's held me here this long. I'll keep in touch and then someday, Sis. . . ."

Two post cards from him, that was all, and they didn't tell much. One from Texas. Another from Oregon. After that, silence. All she had now was the memory of him. Tall, like her; handsome in spite of the slight crook in his nose from when Pa had knocked him over a sawhorse. Cloudy black hair like hers. Like their real father's.

A mourning dove cried far off. A hurting, lonesome sound.

"Why'd you have to go away?" she cried, though she knew. For the same reason she had to go. She seemed to see him standing on shore right where the *Victory* sat above its own rippled reflection. The boat and everything else blurred. She hurried on toward it. Tad would be going along with her in spirit. That was the thing to remember.

"I want a cigar!" Hunch croaked. "I want a cigar, dammit."

She shook the cage. "Oh, shut up, you old fool bird. I shouldn't ever have taken you along. You talk too much. What'll Uncle Stewart think? All those swear words Pa and his cronies taught you." Not only Pa, she thought guiltily. "You ought to try to be nice like Smith. He keeps his mouth shut. But I love you anyhow, for some dumb reason."

Maybe there didn't have to be a reason for loving. Not room to think about that now. There was faithful Smith sunning himself on the prow. Faithful! She didn't trust him out of her sight. But it was true that he kept his mouth shut. She could tell him the deepest, darkest secrets and he would never repeat them to anybody else. Right now he looked sleepy, not a bit excited about the trip. His front legs curled under him so that his knees were like furry, gray-and-white striped knobs.

A bluejay, as blue as a cut-out piece of summer sky,

cried at her from a tree branch. She looked around, wary. A frog plopped. A ring of circles in the water showed where a carp had surfaced and plunged. Not many game fish left. Old tires, like round, rubber animals, poked up along shore.

"The river's the town sewer," Tad had said, worrying.

Blue set Hunch down, tossed supplies into the boat, and leaned over to kiss Smith on his forehead. He lashed his tail as if kissing embarrassed him. The one thing he would not permit was hugging.

"All right, mates," she said, hoisting the cage on board. "I have to hurry back, get a few more things, then we're off." She took time to admire the freshly painted name, *Victory.* She had snitched the white paint from a can Pa had stored in the lean-to, but only Smith and Hunch knew that. Underneath, the old name that Tad had given the boat still showed faintly. The *Mud Hen.*

"Not a proper name for a proud boat," she argued with Tad's silent presence. Tad would understand. The *Victory* was a name for something important, for her and Tad both. Onward and upward. It wasn't really upward in this case since the Chicksaw flowed down toward the Mississippi and they would be sailing south, not north. But onward, certainly, and ever victorious.

A voice near her elbow spoke. "Whatja doin'?"

She whirled. It was only little Tibo, scrawny,

underfed, and big-eyed, hitching up his over-sized pants, a bare toe showing through ragged sneakers. "What're *you* doing away from the Home?"

"I 'scaped."

"You'd better escape right back. You'll get a hiding if they find you gone."

"They don't care. They'd just as soon we'd run off, Kelley says. That way they don't have to feed us."

"Who's Kelley?"

"He's one of the big kids. Going on ten."

"You won't get beyond six if you don't clear out."

He spat, imitating the grown-up snoose chewers. "I'm seven, almost! Though I ain't sure. Mr. Bert ain't either." He picked up a small stone and skipped it across the water as if it were what he had come down to the river for. "I'm runnin' away. What're *you* doin'?"

She met the big, questioning eyes. Far darker than her hair. She did not trust them, innocent though they seemed. He wasn't a bit over six years old, she was certain; just full of brag and lies. Not that she could blame him much, living in the moldy old Home, as the Chicksaw County Shelter for Homeless and Unwanted Children was called. Sometimes she walked by the place and saw Tibo playing with the others in the rough yard enclosed by a high fence. He stood out, somehow. Tad had gone over regularly, coaching games, helping out, practicing to be a social worker some day.

"What I'm doing is my business," she told Tibo. "Now, get lost. I've lots to do."

"I kin help."

"I don't need help."

The almost passionate, eager smile he wore faded. Something dangerously close to tears glimmered in the dark eyes. Indian eyes? Tad had said something about "that little Indian kid. Part Indian, anyhow. Though Tibo doesn't seem an Indian name."

Tibo did have a slightly burnt hue, a bit like the reddish-brown bark of a birch tree when you peeled away the papery white outer sheath. Maybe it was true that he had been left at the Home by somebody up at the Fond du Lac Indian Reservation. "You'd better get back to the Home, Tibo," Blue warned.

"I ain't goin' back. I'm goin' with you. I've been watchin'—you're gettin' ready to go somewheres. I sneak down here lots of times. I've seen you luggin' stuff to this here boat almost every day. Tad told me all about the boat." He gazed at the muddy sand and kicked it with his bare toe. "I like Tad. He was the only one paid much attention to me. Where's he now?"

Blue hesitated. "He went away."

"Where to?"

She cleared her throat against the tightness there. "I guess maybe he went up to Alaska—or some other new place. Wherever, he's probably saving up money so that he can send for me. . . ." She no longer believed in that dream. "Now, I told you—clear out!"

"Ain't gonna. You're runnin' away, too. I know! And I'm goin' with you. If you don't take me I'll go tell." The tears, real or false, glimmered in his eyes again. "Come on. Please, Blue. I kin be a big help, honest!"

She felt trapped: not by his threatened tears—although they made her feel a bit soft—but by his threat. He might just run and blab what he thought he knew.

She played for time, trying to think. "I'm only taking some time off from school for a fishing trip. It's kind of an assignment. Now I have to hurry up and go get some more stuff."

"I'll wait here," Tibo said. He stood where he was, legs spraddled, seeming to take root.

Blueberry glared, then marched off. She would have to find a way to cope with Tibo later.

Onward and Upward

BLUEBERRY EASED THE SCREEN DOOR shut behind her, then stopped short. Her mother sat at the kitchen table staring into space while she stirred a cup of what looked like cold coffee. Beside the cup was one of her love story magazines opened to a picture of a man and woman kissing.

Mrs. Flynn turned toward Blue, plucked eyebrows raised. "What're you ramming around for—not even dressed for school yet."

"Same thing I always wear." Blue rubbed a damp palm against her jeans. Ma didn't usually notice what she wore. "The teacher put me on a special assignment. I'm supposed to camp in the woods all by myself for a whole day and night and then make a written report. I've been setting up camp. Now I have to take a couple of blankets and some food."

Mrs. Flynn blew cigarette smoke out through her nostrils, a gray-blue whiff like a visible snort. "I don't know what gets into teachers, thinking up a silly thing like that!" She waved a narrow hand at the room; the rest of her was growing thick, almost fat, so that her faded robe scarcely fit any more. "This shack is close enough to camping out. Closer than I want to get or ever thought I would."

Blueberry studied her and edged toward the food pantry. Was Ma thinking of when she and Blue's father had been married and lived in a decent kind of house in town? Ma had been Mrs. Thaddeus Lincoln then, not Mrs. Al Flynn.

"I'm not going to have any daughter of mine sleeping in the woods like a tramp. I've a good notion to speak my mind to them teachers."

Blue was not worried. Her mother had never gone as far as the front door of the schoolhouse, not even at Christmas time when Blueberry had a leading role in the pageant. "Ma—why'd you get married again?" she dared to ask.

Her mother breathed another snort of smoke. "How was I suppose to raise two little kids like you and Tad all alone, without any job or money? Answer me that!"

There was a sharp look in her eyes that made

Blueberry hasten to the pantry. She took a slice of bread from the bread box, then spread it with peanut butter. On the sly, she fixed a second one.

"Haven't you already had your breakfast?"

"Yes, but this is for the assignment."

Mrs. Flynn did not comment. She was absorbed, suddenly, in her magazine.

Blueberry read those stories herself sometimes, but she didn't think much of them. People were always falling in love and getting into trouble because of it. Terrible things were always happening, like having babies without real fathers. Blue had decided passionate love was not for her, and she was never going to be married if she could help it.

She glanced toward her mother again, then eyed the canned milk on an upper shelf. Smith turned up his pink nose at milk of any kind, but a growing boy like Tibo. . . . No need to think about him. He would probably have run off, tired of waiting, by the time she returned to the boat. Still, the milk was a handy item. She slipped a few cans and the peanut butter sandwiches into a paper bag, and started to move away toward her room.

Mrs. Flynn looked up. Light through the dusty window made a dull glint on her hair; it was graying at the roots under the dyed blond frizz. Ma must have been pretty once. Sometimes she dressed up for a dance or a party somewhere but that had not happened for a long while. She didn't seem to care much about anything anymore except reading the love magazines and smoking and sipping a can of beer whenever there was money to afford it.

"What're you sneaking out in that bag?" Ma demanded.

"I told you. Rations for camping out."

"The place to eat is here at the table." She pressed her hand to her forehead. "You be back in time to do the dishes, Miss Girl Scout. Get me an aspirin. My head's pounding. Something woke me—I shouldn't have got up so soon. I'm going back to bed."

Blueberry hurried to the cupboard where the aspirin bottle stood, poured a glass full of water, and handed it and the aspirins to her mother. "I hope you'll feel better, Ma, after I—when I get back." She wasn't ever going to come back! Never! Maybe Ma would miss her a little, if only that she wouldn't be around to do the dishes and other chores. "Ma. . . ."

"What now?" Ma gulped the aspirin.

"Nothing," Blue said. "Nothing except. . . ." She dug a sweating fist into the pocket of her jeans. "I wish you were still a Lincoln. That's what I am even though everybody calls me Flynn. Pa's never legally adopted me."

"Flynn's as good a name as any." Her gaze lingered on Blueberry, a shadowy sadness in it, then flicked swiftly to a fly that had settled on the magazine. "Swatter's always someplace else when I need it." She stood up, sighed, and went back to her bedroom.

Blue hesitated, wishing she had dared to say more

or that Ma had said more. Her mother had seemed almost on the edge of saying something—that sudden, sad remembering in her eyes—but the moment had passed. It always did. Ma was in another world somewhere, in her mind, except when she got mad and lashed out at everybody, throwing stuff around so that there was nothing to do but duck and run. Even when she had found the farewell note from Tad the seam of her mouth stayed tight. But the next day, Blue had surprised her reading the note again, and watched her pace up and down the kitchen, half-crying and half-cursing. Blue had managed on the sly to read the note later. It said only, "Dear Ma—I'm going. Have to. Take care of yourself and especially of Blue. She could amount to something even if I never do. Love, Tad."

After her brief outburst Ma went back to being the way she had been before except that her face looked stiffer, as if she had put a mask on.

In her own room, Blueberry looked around for the last time. She opened the scarred dresser's bottom drawer and removed the heart-shaped perfume bottle. A marvel that Pa hadn't smashed it when he had poured all the fragrant contents out into the kitchen sink; she had used hardly more than two drops. The only thing about Pa that was sharp was his sense of smell.

The other treasure, a necklace with beads shining like a dragonfly's wings, remained intact. Tenderly, she placed it and the empty perfume vial into a button-down pocket of the knapsack Tad had once bought at the army surplus store in the city of Brainerd. Using it now made her feel closer to him; maybe he had even purposely left it for her. She rummaged in the closet and in the hiding space under the bed, tucking needed articles into the knapsack. She took special care with Tad's worn dictionary and his harmonica.

Blankets under her arm, an extra jacket, the canvas bag strapped over her shoulders, she stole back to the pantry. Two cans of baked beans stood there as if yearning not to be left alone. She added these to the sack and, as a last inspiration, a cake of dried yeast. Flour was already on board.

There. She was as ready as she would ever be. Still she hesitated, looking toward the closed door of Ma's bedroom, fighting back her feelings. There wasn't anything to be sad about. Ma would either get hopping mad when she found her gone or she would shrug and say, "Blue'll come back when she feels like it." Pa would probably just give an extra hard spit.

The fly was on the magazine again, rubbing its hind legs together. Blue found the fly swatter, took aim, and smashed it. There the squashed thing lay beside big print that read: ONE MOMENT OF RECKLESS PASSION RUINED MY WHOLE LIFE!

Quickly, Blueberry went outside, down the three front steps, and into the weedy, chicken-loud yard. At the last bend of the path, she glanced back, wondering if Tad had felt the same small tug when he left. She went on, resolving to forget Ma, everything. The bright promise of the day started to glow inside her again.

A chipmunk darted across the path. Something larger and furrier bounded into an empty section of a rusted culvert. Blueberry stooped down, peering. A small, round-eyed kitten stared back from its hiding place, imagining that it was safely concealed.

"You silly," she said. "I'll bet you're one of Smith's offspring." Goodness knew how many children, grandchildren, and great-grandchildren Smith could lay claim to. He was always courting some feline ladylove. Blueberry grinned. Smith hadn't learned the awful dangers of reckless passion!

She hurried on, trying to think if she had forgotten anything. She had made careful lists. If she had forgotten some item it was too late now.

The river was shining around the boat. On a rock near shore Old Sludge the mud turtle was sunning himself. His mossy shell looked as if it were covered with wet, green felt. She wouldn't miss him any. Sludge always stole bullheads from her fish stringer when he could.

She looked up and down the shore and let her breath gust out in relief. No Tibo. Smith? Smith was missing! Well, he would turn up once she whistled for him; probably only answering a call of nature.

She climbed on board, dragging her supplies with her, and moved toward the cabin. The cabin was as neat as a duck's tail. Not a lot bigger either, she had to admit. It had sturdy walls and a roof but it was open at both ends. The forward entrance was narrow. The other end, facing the stern, was wide; in bad weather she hung a heavy canvas tarpaulin there to protect the interior. Now the tarp hung over the narrow front opening to conceal the cabin from eyes on shore. She set down her burdens and reached up to remove the tarp. The boat rocked and Tibo leaped out of the cabin, grinning.

"Dammit all, Tibo! D'you want to capsize the ship? What're you doing here? Nobody said you could come on board. This is private property."

"I was just tryin' to learn about things so I'd be more of a help. I'm gonna join the navy when I grow up and maybe I'll even become a captain."

"*If* you grow up, you mean. I've a mind to put you out of your misery right here and now before you bring trouble to the whole crew. Get out of my way—disappear! I have to shove off, and fast!" She cast an apprehensive glance toward shore, half-expecting to see Ma or some tattle-tale schoolmate sneaking out of the tree shadows. She whipped back the tarp and stepped into the cabin, tossing the extra grocery bag down on the small counter near the one-burner kerosene stove.

Tibo followed, dragging blankets. "Where d'you want me to put these, Blue?"

"On the lower bunk there. Bring me that knapsack—and don't sling it around. It's got valuable things inside."

"Yes'm."

"You're supposed to say, 'Aye, aye, sir.' " She took time to stow various articles in place and to inspect the box stored under the bunk. The very special box with its treasure of small, wooden figurines she had carved was safe and sound. She turned to Tibo. "Tibo, I can't take you. Honest. There's not room for more than Smith and Hunch and me."

"I don't take up much room." He tried to look even smaller than he was, hunching his narrow shoulders together. "There was room for you and Tad and he was lots bigger'n me."

"We only took short trips. I don't have enough food for a growing boy. Anyhow, I might have the law on me, helping you to escape from the Home."

"They wouldn't care—I could be a stowaway you didn't even know was here! Please, Blue." The dark eyes burned into hers, begging. "I kin fish good, for extra food. And I'm real handy at peelin' potatoes and things."

She looked away from the pleading eyes. Maybe she could teach him to be a help. A second hand could be very useful at times. Not that she really needed one, she argued with herself. Yet, she heard herself saying, "Well, all right. But don't just stand there. We have to get moving. You sit in the prow there and be ready to catch the tow rope when I toss it up. Did you see where Smith went?"

Tibo straightened, trying now to look as tall as he could. "No, ma'am—no, sir, I mean. Except he lit out after another cat."

Blue's eyes narrowed with suspicion. "Was it a girl cat?"

"I dunno, but it had a tip of its orange tail missin'."

Blueberry groaned. "That's the Browns' cat—has kittens as fast as you can count." She clambered down to shore, whistling for Smith, then untied the tow rope. "Catch!" she called. In his eagerness Tibo reached out too far and almost fell overboard.

She whistled toward the woods again, then yelled, "Come here, John Joseph Jeremiah Smith, blast you! I'll give you exactly one minute. Otherwise—we leave without you, d'you hear?" To make good her threat she moved to the anchor lying on the sand. She lugged the heavy anchor—concrete set in an old pail—toward the boat. Tibo's skinny arms made her glad for her own strong muscles. "You just stand back," she said with a grunt. Blue lowered the anchor pail against the prow crossboard, then started to push the boat toward deeper water. "Move back aft," she commanded Tibo. Straining against the boat, she looked back over her shoulder. "Don't think I'm going to waste any more good breath calling you, Smith!" The keel scraped on sand, then floated free. Blue poised, ready to leap on board, but still looking toward the woods.

Out from the tree shadows sauntered Smith, tail high in the air. He was taking his time. When he was within an arm's distance, Blueberry reached out. She cupped one hand under his ample rear and gave him a boost that sent him sailing across the prow. Smith landed with a soft plop, cast an aggrieved look, then sat down and began to wash one striped hind leg.

Blue gave a final shove and at the same time hoisted herself on board, her sneakers dripping. Cargo and crew were safe, the ripple-shining world ahead. "We're off mates! Onward and upward!" She took a long poling stick from its niche along the gunwales and pushed the boat farther off shore before she made her way through the cabin to the outboard motor fastened at the stern.

"Whatja want me to do now—sir?" Tibo asked.

"Don't hop around. You go into the cabin and duck down there so nobody'll see you. If anybody sees me they'll think I skipped school to go fishing or such. Try to keep a sharp eye on shore. And if you see something suspicious. . . ."

"I wanna be out where I kin look at things better."

"There'll be plenty to see later. You do as I say. I'm the captain here."

"Aye, aye, ma'am—sir." He moved obediently to the small cabin which was approximately midships and crouched there while craning his neck to watch the shoreline, as ordered.

Blueberry pulled the starting cord on the outboard motor. Two tries and it chugged into life. She glanced at gear and cargo again, making doubly sure that all was in order. The cans of extra gasoline were snug under the stern seat, the oars carried for emergency were strapped upright against one outside cabin wall, a small fire extinguisher alongside.

There was no sign of movement on shore except for Old Sludge sliding back into the water.

"I don't see nothin' yet," Tibo called from the cabin. He ventured toward the wide opening that faced Blue.

"Stay back there—we aren't all clear yet."

It took only a few minutes to reach the middle of the river where the current helped the *Victory* on its way. Blue set the outboard's throttle at medium speed and relaxed, one hand resting loosely on the tiller. Even Tibo could guide the boat in such a placid stream. The current here was lazy, scarcely strong enough to sail a leaf on although the little water striders near shore never seemed to make any head-way against it. For every stride the stilt-legged bugs made forward, the river carried them back the same distance so that they were forever walking in one place. Still, if they did not keep moving they would have no hope at all. There was a lesson in that, she reflected. If she simply stayed in Chicksaw Landing and didn't try to get ahead in life she would end up farther back than where she had started.

"Kin I come out pretty soon?" Tibo asked.

"Wait 'til we're out beyond the trestle. Sometimes the school kids walk on it to prove how brave they are. It's dangerous. If a train comes whoosing along there's no place to go except jump down into the river and maybe end up on the rocks."

"I'd dare to do it! But I ain't ever been that far. Have you done it, Blueberry?"

"Sure." She had, twice, to prove to herself that she could.

The lean shadow of the railroad trestle swept over them, tracks empty. Then, beyond, there was mostly flat, lonely country, the little town of Chicksaw Landing almost lost in the middle of the scrub except for the church steeple sticking up like a white, witch's hat, and the water tank on its tall, metal legs. Here and there a gnarled spire of a white pine the early lumberjacks had left reared up over the second- and third-growth jackpines. Remains of giant stumps had rotted away to the color of old bone. Where land had been burned over, blueberry thickets sprouted.

The stream widened and deepened. Blue inhaled the sweet-sour smell of the river and listened to the wave-lisp against the keel.

"We're on our way, Tad," she whispered.

"Who're you talkin' to?" Tibo asked from the cabin.

"Myself." It was almost the truth. She and Tad had been so close in spite of his being seven years older. She looked toward little Tibo hunched in the cabin, his eyes as big as black dollars. It wasn't too bad to see him there.

"You can come out now," she said, and turned her face to the distant horizon, feeling the wind on her cheeks. She watched a blue heron far off flap upward, its long legs trailing behind like something it had almost forgotten to take along.

River Dreams

"WE'RE GOIN' PRETTY FAST, AIN'T we?" Tibo sat facing Blueberry. For a full ten minutes he had managed to stay almost quiet except for jerking around once in a while to point at some abandoned shack as if it were an exciting castle, or to a stray dog that he was certain was a wolf. "Will we be goin' even faster when we reach the big river?"

"Fast enough." Blueberry brushed a wind-whipped lock of hair from her eyes, keeping her other hand on the tiller. "What's your hurry?"

'I ain't hurryin'. Where're you goin', Blue?"

"How come you're so nosey all of a sudden? You didn't ask anything about where we were going when you forced me to take you along."

"I didn't think about it, then. I was only thinkin' of goin' with you."

Blueberry looked solemn as she recalled what her favorite teacher Miss Holm had once said. "You have to learn in life," Blue quoted in a teacherly voice, "that dashing off without thinking where you're going is very foolish. If you don't have a goal in mind, you could end up being a drifter."

"What's a drifter?"

"You know, somebody who just drifts from place to place, not really getting anywhere." Like Tad? No, not clever Tad. But what if something had happened to him? She pushed the thought away.

Tibo's interest shifted abruptly. "Hey, where's the toilet on this boat?"

"Most of the time we have to go on shore. But in an emergency or if it's storming, there's a pot under the lower berth, and a canvas curtain you can pull. Do you have to go already?"

"Nope. I was just wonderin'."

"You're a boy. That makes it a lot easier to do number one."

Tibo looked thoughtful. "When're we gonna eat? I'm starvin'."

"At about two bells; by then we'll be completely out

of sight and sound of anything to do with Chicksaw Landing."

"What's two bells?"

"It's how ship people tell time." She wasn't herself sure how this was reckoned.

"Oh. Well, I'm still starvin'. They didn't let me have no breakfast."

"What did you do that you shouldn't?"

He grinned, showing a missing eyetooth. "I pinned a toilet paper tail on Missus Platt. She's the head cook. I took a long strip and stuck it through the top of her skirt belt while she was busy." He covered his mouth with his hand and giggled. "And then she went marchin' around the big kitchen with the paper tail flyin' out behind her, and the kids was all laughin' until she knowed something was wrong."

"*Knew,*" Blue corrected. But it wasn't her responsibility to try and educate Tibo. When they reached the city he would have to make out for himself, somehow. She would try to help though, and Uncle Stewart would too. Still: "That wasn't very nice, making fun of the cook like that."

"She's mean. She whacked me with a potato masher once—and I bit her!" He looked proud. "I could eat a potato masher right now."

"Oh, all right! There're some crackers in a carton near the burner. You can have a couple but don't eat the whole lot. Give Hunch a piece of one."

"What if he bites me again?"

"Again?"

"When I was waitin' for you to come back to the boat I put my finger in his cage to pet him and he nipped me hard."

"Serves you right." Her grin was sly. "He likes a nip of meat now and then."

Tibo went into the cabin. He opened the box of crackers and glanced back to see if she was watching. She was. He took out two and a half crackers, gingerly poking the latter through the bars of Hunch's cage. He returned, munching. "A person can't whistle right after eatin' crackers. When're you gonna teach me how to steer this here boat?"

"Who said I ever was?" She had been thinking how easy it would be on this quiet stretch of river for Tibo to man the tiller while she did other chores. But he didn't have to know that.

"I could learn fast. I've been watchin'."

"It isn't as simple as it looks. But—well, you watch hard now. To steer to the right, turn the tiller this way. Left, go the opposite. Otherwise, on a straight course, you mostly hold it steady."

"I kin do it, Blue! Just let me try oncet."

"*Once*. Don't you know anything?"

He shrugged. "I kin read—some."

She studied the river again. There was no rock or visible snag anywhere. "All right. Come and sit beside me. Now, take a firm hold, and always keep your eyes on what's ahead."

His small hand was as fragile-looking as a bird's brown claw against the black rubber handle. If Tibo really had Indian blood, perhaps steering a boat would come as easily to him as steering a canoe had been for his ancestors—if they had been lake and river Indians here in northern Minnesota. She guided his hand at first, then let him take over.

"More to the right," she coached.

He swung the tiller sharply.

"Not so far, dummy! You're making us wobble all over the place. Ah-h-h, give it to me! I'm going to put you to work peeling potatoes and swabbing decks."

"I'm not either a dummy!" His underlip was unsteady. "You didn't hardly give me a chance."

"Stop blubbering. Here." She removed her hand from the tiller. "Try again but if you can't do it right we'll have to anchor while I fix some lunch, and we'll lose precious time."

He gripped the tiller, mouth clenched in determination, eyes fixed straight ahead.

Hunch squawked loudly, "Did somebody let a poop?"

Tibo snickered.

Blue clicked her teeth. If the parrot talked like that around Uncle Stewart, she would die! It was so important that Uncle Stew would like her. But what if she couldn't find him? Her chin firmed. She would find him. She had to.

In the galley, she commanded Hunch, "Shut your beak." She opened a can of milk, thinned it with water, and mixed in some cocoa she had saved for a special treat on board. There were two hard-boiled eggs. Those and sandwiches would do, she decided, until they reached port tonight. Then they'd have a hot meal.

Over her shoulder she called to Tibo, "If you see a floating snag, or a rock, or another boat, yell."

"Aye, aye," he responded, gaze glued to the river.

Smith appeared and rubbed himself against her leg.

"You hungry too, honey? When we drop anchor tonight you can go ashore and rustle up some wild food. 'Til then you'll have to wait."

Hunch hollered, "Pass the spuds!"

Blueberry dipped into the sack of scraps she'd been able to save. If she ran out of "parrot food," Hunch would have to live off whatever wild seeds she could find on land.

She tossed a bit of her peanut butter sandwich to Smith. He inspected it, sniffed in disdain, and walked off.

Back in the stern, Blue took over the tiller, while she and Tibo shared the sandwiches, eggs, and cocoa.

"Boy, this is real good!" Tibo acclaimed, sipping from his tin mug. "This is a real neat ship, too. And now that I'm learnin' to steer so good I bet you're glad you took me along, huh?"

"Depends. Things may not be so easy all the rest of the way."

"They ain't so easy at the Home either. What're *you* runnin' away for, Blue?"

"I'm going to make something of myself, not rot

away in Chicksaw Landing like most everybody else there. I told you about having a goal in life. Well, I've got one." She gestured. "I hate almost everything back there, and nobody cares about me. Not even Ma. Tad and I planned this trip but we were going even farther, way down to New Orleans maybe. He and I are both Lincolns, you know. You've heard of Abe Lincoln, haven't you?"

"Sure. He was a President, and he got shot."

"One of the greatest Presidents, and I'm related to him! I've got Presidential blood in my veins."

"What color is it?" Tibo was pointing toward shore. "Ain't that a train way off there? Didja ever ride on a train? I did." He considered. "Or maybe I only dreamed it. Dreams can seem awful real."

"Dreams are the most real things of all," she said. Or was that another kind of lie? It was hard to tell truth from falsehood sometimes. She gave her attention to the outboard and set the speed up a notch. "The sky's beginning to cloud over. You carry the cups back to the galley, mate."

By late afternoon the clouds resembled gray, curdled milk, and the water had a greasy appearance. All the earlier shininess was gone, as if the mucky river bottom had decided to float to the surface. She hated using the water even to wash the dishes but she had to save their drinking water as much as possible. It was hard to know when and where they could refill the large, plastic jug. At a clear, fresh creek, maybe, although Tad said there weren't many unpolluted creeks around. Well, it would be all right if she boiled the water, though that was a chore and used extra fuel.

A neat ship, Tibo had said. Right. Especially the galley, she thought, studying it as she held the tiller steady. All those clever compartments and shelves she and Tad had built, the little stove, the rack for pots and pans. Some of the pans they had picked up at the town dump, pounding out dents with a soft-head hammer. Everything was snug and tight, including the two bunks built along the side opposite the cooking department.

"Is it gonna storm?" Tibo asked.

"Could be." Smith was fidgeting and she knew why. She had put a pan of sand on board for him to use for his private bathroom, but so far he had merely studied it with scorn.

"We'd better take time to put ashore a little while," she told Tibo. "Smith has to go. He's too stubborn to use his pan." Easier to blame Smith, she thought guiltily, than to admit her own need.

"I peed already," Tibo announced, looking smug. "When you was fixin' the cocoa."

"So, what's so great about that? There's a nice slanty shoreline over there to starboard. When I'm ready to land, you stand at attention."

Tibo jerked himself upright, making the boat rock.

"Not yet. Sit down until I give the command!"

Tibo muttered, "You're even bossier than Missus Platt."

"Somebody has to be in—authority." She felt pleased at having found the right word. Miss Holm said she had a good vocabulary and that her grammar was commendable; another lovely word, meaning good. Ma's grammar had been good too, once, but now she was beginning to fall into the habit of the kind of sloppy grammar Pa used.

The water was deep near the sloping shore, with no threatening rocks. Blueberry shut off the motor. Using one of the oars, she stroked until the boat scratched bottom. She removed her shoes, rolled up her jeans, and jumped out. The water reached to her knees. Pulling the tow rope, she called to Tibo, "Give it an extra shove with the pole."

Tibo tried but the *Victory* did not budge.

"Okay. Jump out. I'll take care of the anchor. Do you know how to swim?"

"I can dog paddle." He looked nervous, eyeing the water.

"Smith can cat paddle but he hates getting wet." She studied Tibo. "Are you afraid of water?"

"I ain't afraid of nothing."

"That's a double negative, which means you're afraid of everything. Come on, Smith."

Smith leaped from the prow onto her shoulder, and from there made another long leap onto land. Too late she remembered she had meant to tie a rope around his neck.

Tibo kicked off his sneakers. Taking a deep breath, he lowered himself into the river and shivered. The water came nearly to his waist. "My pants are all wet."

"Why didn't you just take them off?"

"I don't have nothin' on underneath. Hey, it's all slimy on the bottom—and maybe there's a big hole I'll fall into." He stopped where he was.

"I thought you weren't afraid of anything."

"I ain't!" He clenched his teeth and splashed to shore.

"Good. Unless you're in a rush you stay here and guard the boat." She followed in the direction Smith had gone.

In a secluded spot among the trees, she unzipped her jeans. It's lovely here, she thought. Small wildflowers brightened a thick, cool growth of fern. Some of the ferns were spring-new, curled at the ends like little green worms. A mosquito whined past her ear. Another drilled into her wrist. She swatted. "Pesky things."

She looked around for Smith and saw him busily scooping out a hole in some leaf mold. Politely, she turned her back and waited. When she looked again, he was raking soil over the spot.

"All right, honey. Back on board now."

Smith ignored her, inspecting every root and twig. He paused, gazing back in the direction of Chicksaw Landing. Cats cared more about places than they did people, Tad had said. She had heard about cats as well as dogs who had traveled hundreds of miles to return to their homes. If that's what smarty Smith had in mind . . . !

She strode to him, taking him by surprise, and slung him up on her shoulder, holding his whiskery cheek against hers. "You forget all about Chicksaw Landing. We're going to have a new home—you and I—in Minneapolis. We're going to have to learn city ways at Uncle Stewart's. First, I'm going to fix you up with a collar and a leash."

Tibo was waiting on shore, guarding the boat.

"D'you need to go to the woods too?" she asked.

"I only got off because I thought we was gonna stay here long enough to cook some supper."

"Too early yet. You hurry back on board now and I'll hand Smith up to you."

Tibo studied the short span of water between him and the *Victory*, then, grim-faced, waded in. When he was safe in the prow, Blueberry handed Smith over.

Smith fought against Tibo's clutching hands. "I can't hold him!" Tibo cried just as Smith wriggled free and dashed off to the stern.

Blue shoved the boat free, hauled herself on board, and using the pole pushed until they were in deeper water.

"He scratched me!" Tibo complained.

"You'll be lucky if you don't have more than a scratch before this journey is through. Pull the tow rope up, then coil it neat." She started the outboard.

"You take over the tiller again. I've some studying to do."

"My arm's tired from steerin'—and the scratch hurts."

"If you don't stop whining I'm going to toss you overboard and it'll be either sink or swim. If you make shore you can trot right back to the Home where they'll be waiting for you with a big paddle."

He sat down and gripped the tiller, downcast and brooding.

She looked at his scratch. It wasn't big but it did have a little blood on it. She had to remember, she told herself, that he was little and frightened in spite of his boasts. She got a Band-Aid and said, "Hold out your arm."

He gazed down at the small strip of tape she fastened there. "That makes it feel better already."

"All right. When it grows dark we'll put into port somewhere, have a meal, and get a good night's rest. We'll need all our strength because if my reckoning's right we'll reach the Little Skunk tomorrow, and that can be a mean river."

Tibo's heavily lashed eyes fixed on her. "I guess you know a lot about life and things, huh?"

"Some," she admitted. She left for the cabin and took Tad's log book from a cubby hole. He had once written deep thoughts into it, even poems, but also scores from when they had played cribbage on board. She wasn't much of a hand at writing but she was good at drawing and whittling. She felt in her pocket. Her jackknife was safely there. It felt solid in her hand and she knew its blades were sharp because she always kept them so. She had whittled objects out of wood ever since she could remember: squirrels, birds, deer, kittens. She had given a kitten figure to Miss Holm.

"Linda," Miss Holm had said, "you have a true artistic talent. Perhaps someday you'll be a famous sculptor and make us all proud."

Blueberry sighed. Everything depended on her finding Uncle Stewart Lincoln. When the perfume and beads arrived two Christmases ago she had written to him but she could not be certain of the address. It was either 2534 Garfield or Fairfield; the writing had blurred from snow. Her letter had come back, undelivered. Ma, when Blue asked her, shrugged. "I don't know where he is. No point in keeping in touch. Your father did. They were close and I guess Stewart was pretty well-to-do. But that's a long time ago, before your dad died."

Being well-to-do, Blue reflected, meant having plenty of money, like the town mayor. His house was the nicest in Chicksaw, with a gorgeous lawn and a paved driveway. Probably Uncle Stewart's would be twice as fine. She wished she had something better to wear than the almost new jeans and clean, checked blouse she was saving for when they met.

She looked through the small cabin window at the

sky. Windy, dirty-looking clouds. She leafed through the log book and took a map from a drawer. With a pencil she circled the spot where the Chicksaw River flowed into the Little Skunk, then on to where the Little Skunk emptied into White Wing Lake before it flowed out again on the other side. White Wing was large and treacherous.

She chewed on the pencil, trying to calculate nautical miles. There was a jolt; a yell from Tibo.

Blue hurried to the stern. "What's wrong—what did you do?"

"I didn't do nothin'! There was a little stub of wood floatin' off side and I steered past it, only. . . ."

There was a bumping, scraping noise directly below the stern. She pushed past him, staring. "Your little stub was part of a big log!" She raised the outboard so it wouldn't be smashed. "Hand me an oar. Quick!"

He did as he was told, crying, "I didn't see no log!"

"Well, you can see it now!" She thrust the oar down against the floating log. "Stubborn brute," she panted, giving a harder thrust. Suddenly, the log drifted free. She leaned over the side. There were no visible signs of damage except for some scraped paint, but she felt shaken as she sank down on the steering seat. "I ought to send you to bed without any supper at all. You have to use your head as well as your eyes."

"I was tryin' to, damn it all!" he blurted. Tears shot from his eyes as if fired by a water pistol. "You're meaner, even, than Missus Platt. I thought you'd be nice—like Tad."

"You settle down now—and no more swearing."

"You swear plenty!"

"So what?" she snapped. "But we'd both better watch it. Especially around Uncle Stewart."

Tibo pressed one hand to his midriff. "I got an awful cramp."

He did look pale. Visions of a mortally ill Tibo worried her. "You go lay—lie—down. Maybe you need a good physic."

Tibo looked wary. "It ain't that. It's that whenever something bad happens, I get sick. Sometimes I throw up. Mr. Bert says it's because I'm very high strung."

"Well, throw up overboard, not on deck. Then lie down for a while. I know you didn't mean to hit the log," she added less harshly.

Tibo crept onto the lower bunk and there was silence except for the throbbing outboard motor, and Hunch squawking nonsense to himself.

Blueberry set the throttle low and tied the tiller in a central position, leaving the boat to itself for a moment while she tiptoed into the cabin. Tibo lay quietly on the lower bunk.

"Are you all right?"

He mumbled, "Yeah—guess so."

Blue took the map, thrust it into her hip pocket, and returned to the stern. There she studied the map again, tracing the rivers to the Mississippi with her forefinger. Following a river was not like following a road because rivers wound back and forth on themselves as if they didn't have any sense of direction. Well, there was food enough on board for a week, if they were careful. Once they reached Uncle Stewart's they wouldn't need to worry.

She wondered what he looked like. Tall and handsome, probably, like her father in the picture taken not long before he was killed in the accident at the logging camp.

Smith jumped up into her lap. She stroked him, listening to his purr that was like a little, humming saw. Sometimes, when he was at the edge of sleep, he sounded like a teakettle on the boil.

"I'll bet Uncle Stew will be surprised when we show up," she told Smith. "I only hope he likes me—us. I know I'm going to like him. And you'd better too. He's my dad's older brother, you know."

She swung the tiller slightly, correcting the course. Ma had said, "The last I heard of your uncle he lived down in Springfield. Must have moved to Minneapolis, judging by the postmark on the package you got."

Springfield, Illinois, naturally. That was where Abe Lincoln had lived when he became a senator. Tad's dictionary had once belonged to their father; his name was written in it: Thaddeus Lincoln, Springfield. The back pages of the dictionary said the name Thaddeus meant "Praise to God." Her own name, Linda, was

Spanish according to the book and meant "beautiful."

"I hate my looks," she had confided to her mother once.

"You could look a lot better if you'd ever fix your hair," Ma had answered.

Smith sat purring in her lap, opening and closing his claws on her thigh. Kneading bread, Blueberry called it.

"Yessir, Uncle Stewart's going to get a surprise. I hope he won't be mad. Maybe he won't even remember me or sending me the presents."

One of Smith's claws pierced the denim of her jeans.

"Blast you, John Joseph Jeremiah Smith!"

There was a sudden twist to the river ahead. She dumped Smith from her lap and applied herself to navigating.

As she was making the turn, a voice called from near shore. She turned to see a sunburned man wearing a straw hat, fishing with a cane pole from a rowboat.

"Howdy!" the man called. "That's quite a rig you got there. Where're you heading?"

"Just down river a ways—my father and me—I."

Tibo came out of the cabin, hauling at his drooping trousers. "Who you talkin' to, Blueberry?"

"Just a fisherman." To the man she said lamely, "He's my little brother. Well, good fishing."

The *Victory* moved on and Blueberry thought the

man watched them with a suspicious gaze. If anybody happened to be looking for her and Tibo, the man would be able to tell what he had seen.

She tried to shrug off anxiety. A person couldn't worry about everything that came along, especially when there were many bigger things to worry about.

"How do you feel?" she asked Tibo.

"Better. When're we gonna eat again? I'm starvin'."

"Everybody has to earn their grub here. Since you're feeling so good, you can take your turn at the tiller."

"Smith and Hunch don't do nothin' for their grub."

"Hunch can't. He's in a cage. And Smith doesn't have any mice to catch here on shipboard. He earns his keep plenty, around home. He's the greatest mouser in Chicksaw. Uncle Stewart can probably use a good mouser too, unless he has servants to catch them."

"Who's Uncle Stewart?"

"My uncle, obviously. You sit down here and take my place while I study things some more."

Tibo took over the tiller. "You know somethin', Blue? Hunch is beginnin' to like me. I gave him another piece of cracker and he took it right out of my fingers without tryin' to bite."

"How did you get another cracker?"

"Uh, well, I—it fell out of the box, from before, I guess. It was just layin' there, so I gave it to Hunch."

"After you ate most of it yourself! Stealing and lying

are sins. You be careful or I'll make you walk the plank."

"What's that mean?"

"It's what pirates did when they wanted to get rid of somebody for good."

In the prow she studied the lay of the land and the still-curdled sky. A wind was springing up now, out of the north, bringing a chill with it, and a hint of rain. It would be smart to find a snug port before wind or rain grew really serious, then take time for a hearty supper.

Smith jumped up on the prow, looking toward shore.

"I know what's in your scheming little brain, Smith." She returned to the cabin, seeking a narrow rope to fashion into a collar and leash.

"I want a cigar! Dammit!" Hunch rasped.

Dreamily, she wondered if Uncle Stewart smoked cigars. What if she never found him?

She shook the thought away and set her chin in what Ma called its stubborn line. It was good to be stubborn when you wanted the right thing.

Stranger at Dusk

"THAT WAS A NEAT SUPPER, BLUE." Tibo sat back from the dying campfire, rubbing his belly in satisfaction. "Are we gonna camp out here to-night? I never camped out before."

"No. Not with snug bunks on board." Blueberry put the leftover beans and corned beef in a bag for Hunch. "I told you the reason we came ashore was mostly to cook over an open fire to save the kero-sene."

Tibo stood up, scratching a mosquito bite. He hopped over a nearby stump a few times as if he were playing leapfrog, then pointed. "Hey, what's that?"

Blueberry glanced toward the weathered sign at the edge of a pine clump. "Just something somebody put up a long time ago and forgot about."

"What's it say?"

"No trespassing. Keep out, in other words. But it's nothing to worry about. We're not doing anything wrong and there probably isn't a house within miles. Whoever does own this land should be glad we cleared out some of the dead wood. It's a fire hazard. Only, we have to be sure to put out our own fire now. If you want exercise so much, go haul a pail full of water from the river and dump it on the embers. And toss this bag of food scraps on board. I'm going to see how Smith is doing."

Smith, tied to a tree, was not doing very well. He had wound his rope tether around and around the trunk so that he had little freedom left. With his ears laid back against his head, he fought at the rope collar.

"D'you want to choke yourself to death?" Blue knelt beside him. "If you'd behave yourself you wouldn't have to be a captive. Here now, let me unwind you. Then I'll take you for a nice walk."

Freed from the tree, Smith still fought the leash, lunging against the collar so hard that he had a coughing fit. Treating Smith as a prisoner was not going to work. He had been a free-roaming creature all his life. He looked up at her now as if to ask what he had ever done to deserve such treatment.

"It's for your own good, sweetie," she told him, but she felt guilty.

Suddenly, Smith bristled and arched his back.

Blueberry turned to see a small black and white fox terrier. The dog bounced forward, wagging its stump of a tail. Smith crouched, hissed, then leaped, tearing the end of the leash from Blueberry's grasp. Before she could blink, he disappeared into the forest shadows, the terrier racing behind him.

She stood where she was, alarmed by more than Smith's escape. The terrier obviously belonged to someone and that "someone" was approaching, a menacing silhouette against the fading sunlight.

"What're you doing here?" the stranger demanded.

"I. . . ." Blueberry cleared her throat, peering. The voice sounded like a woman's. Now she saw that the stranger *was* a woman in spite of her man's overalls and felt, slouch hat.

"I—we were only having some supper," Blueberry stammered. "Then I was just going to take Smith—he's my cat—for a short walk before going back on shipboard."

"Shipboard? What Ship? Didn't you see my sign, or can't you read?"

"Yes, ma'am. We were only resting from the boat—it's my boat, ma'am—and we weren't hurting anything."

The woman looked toward the cook fire. A spark, lashed by a gust of wind, flew toward the trees. "See that. With the woods as dry as they are you could start a forest fire."

Tibo appeared, lugging a pail of water from the

river. Without looking toward Blue and the stranger he splashed water on the fire's coals. A column of smoke and steam rose. "Hey, Blueberry," he called into the gloom. "Is that enough?"

"Blueberry?" the woman echoed. She pushed her hat back as if to gain a closer look at Blue, revealing a gaunt face and bristling, gray eyebrows. "Blueberry what? Where do you live?"

"Blueberry Lincoln, ma'am. I live—uh, near Brush Falls." Brush Falls was some twenty miles up river from Chicksaw Landing. "Please, we were just leaving—that is, we were going to spend the night on our ship that's moored here and then sail on in the morning. First, could I look for my cat? He's part of the crew, and very important."

Tibo trotted toward them, straining to see through the shadows. "Who're you talkin' to, Blue?"

"To me," the woman answered, taking a step forward. "And who are you? Another important member of the crew?"

Tibo, stiff-faced, silent, edged close to Blue.

Blueberry drummed up her courage. "He's my little brother, that's who. And it's your dumb dog's fault my cat ran off! We don't need your scrubby old harbor for our ship. We'll shove off and find a place where people aren't so fussy."

"My, my! Spunky one, aren't you?" The woman strode down to the shore and saw the *Victory*. "So that's what you call your ship." Wind blew salt-colored hair out from under her broad-brimmed hat. A spatter of rain fell.

Blue whispered to Tibo. "You keep out of sight. I have to go find Smith." She started off. Desperately, she whistled, then begged, "Smith! Please, Smith, come on!"

The terrier was yapping excitedly. Blueberry ran blindly through thickets of brush, following the sound. The terrier was racing back and forth at the base of a tamarack. Smith was about eight feet up the tree, his rope leash caught on a stub. Blue found a foothold on a lower branch and reached up, straining. Her right hand closed on one of Smith's forelegs. With a gasp she pulled him free and down into her arms.

"Get away!" she yelled at the dog, kicking the air. "It's all right, Smith, pet," she crooned to the hissing, struggling bundle of fur. "We're leaving. In a few minutes everything will be smooth sailing again."

Tibo darted out of the shadows. "What're we gonna do now, Blue?" He gestured toward the tall woman still standing on shore.

"Go right on past her. You climb on board. I'll take care of the rest."

The woman came toward them.

"You can't go out in stormy weather like this, in the dark," she said. "I'll let you stay here for the night, but then you clear out at dawn. I don't want any two kids hanging around here, especially runaways which is what you so obviously are. I don't want the law breathing down my neck."

Blueberry clutched Smith closer. "We're not

runaways. We're going to see my—our—uncle in Minneapolis. He's expecting us."

"A likely story." She looked back at the boat. "That doesn't look very leakproof to me. Do you have blankets? And food?"

"Of course! And the *Victory* is as snug as a bear in a rug. We'll shove off, as I said. I don't need favors from anybody." She started toward the boat, head high, still carrying Smith. Tibo darted ahead.

The terrier was beside the woman now, seeking the protection of her long legs. "If you two go out in that tub tonight you'll founder. They'll say mean old Lena Finch sent two children off to their deaths. You stay right here tonight. What you do from then on is your own business."

Blueberry tried not to show her relief. "Okay, if you insist, Tibo and I'll stay. Now I'd better get Smith here on board and try to feed him some leftovers from our supper. He didn't have a chance to hunt."

"I have a little extra milk I could spare," the woman said.

"Thank you, but he won't touch the stuff. But Tibo—my brother—could stand some. All we have is a few cans of condensed."

Lena Finch studied Tibo in the wan light. "I haven't heard that name, 'Tibo,' since I left New Mexico years ago. It was common among the Spanish-Americans there." She looked from Tibo to Blueberry. "I never saw a brother and sister look less alike. Well, hurry aboard before you're soaked. I'll be back." With that, she walked off, the dog trotting at her heels.

Tibo gazed after her. "I wonder where she lives. Man! I thought she was gonna kill us when she first showed up. Maybe she will when she comes back. Maybe she's gonna get a gun or a knife."

"Stop scaring yourself and get busy. We have to batten down the hatches in case there's a real blow."

Tibo regarded her wonderingly. "I guess that's real sailor talk, like 'two bells,' huh? Are you gonna join the navy, too, when you grow up?"

"I am grown up. Almost. They don't like girls for real sailors on their big ships like on destroyers and aircraft carriers. Come on—there's no time for gabbing."

They crossed the makeshift gangplank.

On board, Blueberry tied Smith inside the cabin. "As soon as we're on our way tomorrow, I'll take off your rope. Cross my heart." She would have to; otherwise his spirit would be broken and he might even come to hate her. Being hated by people wasn't nearly as hard as being hated by Smith or even by Hunch.

She lit the kerosene lantern and hung it from a ceiling hook.

Tibo, hunched on the edge of the lower bunk, looked up at the lantern's orange glow. "That makes things a lot brighter, don't it? At the Home they don't have any lights at night at all except the big yard light. I hate it when everything's dark. Gives me the creeps."

"The only light we'll have after I blow this out is

what's in the sky, and that's not much on a night like this." A thin rain started to fall. She pulled the tarp across the cabin opening and tied it in place.

"I'm awful thirsty," Tibo complained. "Kin I have a cup of water?"

"You're always thirsty or hungry. All right, one cup. We're already running short of water." She looked out at the shore. A faint light pricked the darkness. From the woman's house? "Maybe I should take the water jug and find her," Blueberry mused aloud. The light moved and bobbed, coming closer, and she realized it was a flashlight.

Lena Smith approached, shining the light on board. She paused at the gangplank. "I'm not risking my brittle bones lugging this stuff up to you. You come down here and get it."

Tibo warned in a whisper, "Maybe it's a trick."

Blueberry decided to take the risk. If she could outrun Pa she could outrun somebody who looked to be a lot older. She crossed the gangplank cautiously.

The woman held out a covered bucket and something wrapped in a newspaper. "You can leave the milk bucket on shore when you leave in the morning."

"We will, thank you," Blue promised. She peered in under the newspaper wrapping and sniffed. Cornmeal bread! "Oh, thanks, Mrs. Finch. That's real nice of you."

"*Miss* Finch. I've never been married and don't plan to be."

"Then you're just like me! I know all about the

dangers of reckless passion."

Lena Finch regarded her thoughtfully, one corner of her mouth lifting in what Blueberry was certain was almost a smile. Miss Finch turned away, saying only, "You keep dry now. No need to tell anybody you saw me. I live very privately."

"No, ma'am, I won't." The rain, still a small drizzle, settled on her forearms. "One other thing, Miss Finch, if you please. We're almost out of drinking water."

Lena Finch waved a hand. "There's a fine natural spring bubbling out of some shore rocks only about a hundred paces to starboard. You'll be able to find it easily in the morning."

Starboard. "Have you been on ships?"

"Some. When I was young." She left, hurrying against the increasing rain.

Later, Blueberry stretched out insofar as was possible in the short, narrow bunk, looking out into the rainy night. Surprising how much light there was in spite of the clouds. There must be a moon behind it all. "How're you doing?" she called up to Tibo.

"I was just thinkin' about that good cornmeal bread and milk. Is there any left?"

"Some. For breakfast."

He was silent a moment. "I thought sure she was gonna pull some trick on us—maybe poison us."

"You have to trust somebody in life."

"I don't trust nobody."

"What about me?"

"Well—yeah, I guess. Only, you won't tell me where we're goin' or about your uncle or anything. Is he hidin' out from the fuzz, or in jail?"

"In jail!" Blueberry snorted. "I should say not! He lives in a fine, big house in Minneapolis. He's just waiting for me to show up."

Tibo's voice sounded small, as if squeezed down by the cabin's roof. "He ain't expectin' me, though." He paused. "Unless you tell him I'm your brother, like you did the fisherman."

"I only did that because I had to. Uncle Stew would know better. Even so, I wouldn't ever lie to him. I'll tell him the truth—that we're, well, shipmates."

"I bet he won't like me, though. Nobody does."

Blue let her breath out in impatience. "You'd better just roll over and go to sleep, Tibo. I never heard so much self-pity in my life. Maybe you don't do anything to make people like you."

"Wouldn't make no difference. Everytime I do like somebody a little they get sick or die or turn out to be real crumbs."

"The lady who gave us the corn bread, Miss Finch," Blue murmured, "I bet she was the daughter of a sea captain once. Then through no fault of her own she lost most of her money and had to move to a little house in the woods, with a cow, and a neat vegetable garden, with shining bright pots on the kitchen wall, and flowers in the window. I mean, that's how I picture it even though we haven't really seen it."

Tibo was silent except for deep, sleeping breaths.

Uncle Stewart's place would be even nicer than Miss Finch's. There might even be servants.

Blue turned over. Tomorrow would be a long, hard day, especially if the rain kept falling.

Sleep squirmed away from her. She tried to imagine herself walking up to her uncle's door. Uncle Stew would take one look at the necklace gleaming around her neck, and he would remember at once.

Oh, it was pleasant to lie here and dream about the future, far, far from Chicksaw Landing and the people there who seemed to do nothing but stand around.

When I'm grown-up and famous, I'll send Ma money to join me, she thought.

Hunch stirred in his cage, seeming to cuss even in his sleep. Smith, curled at her feet, was twitching his legs. Did birds or cats dream? She was certain Smith did for she had seen his eyes roll until the whites showed.

"I'll let you go free tomorrow, Smith," she whispered. "I'm going to trust you from now on." Safer than trusting in people, no matter what she had told Tibo.

She burrowed deeper under the blanket, beginning to sink into sleep, lulled by the faint motion of the boat, the soft beat of the rain on the cabin's roof. One tiny leak dripped rain against the head of her bunk. A minor matter.

Goodnight, Tad. She moved her lips soundlessly, then turned over again, carefully, so as not to disturb Smith.

Sleepless Night

REDDISH LIGHT SHONE FAINTLY through the boat's cabin, and although wind still rippled the tarp there was no sound of rain.

Blueberry swung her legs over the bunk, pulled her jeans on over her panties, and called up to Tibo. "Time to get up!"

There was no response.

She reached up and shook the blanket-covered huddle. "Tibo! Wake up!"

He jerked awake, looking about him in confused alarm before he realized where he was. "I was havin' a real nice dream. What did you have to go and spoil it for?" He fumbled for his clothes at the foot of the bunk.

Blue portioned out their breakfast and said, "You can have half of the milk and half of the corn bread. We'll fix something more later but now we have to get ready to leave."

Tibo stood beside her. "I'm freezin' to death."

She reached into a crowded compartment and drew out the extra jacket she had brought. "Here. This was Tad's when he was young."

He drew it on. "Honest, did Tad once wear it? It fits me good, don't it."

"It's okay." It was several sizes too large.

Smith rubbed himself against her leg, making plaintive, hungry meows. She had one can of cheap cat food. Now was as good a time as any to open it. She found a can opener, then spooned a portion onto a saucer.

Smith ate greedily and waited for more.

"You can go hunt your own food while there's a chance. Then, if you can't find any I'll let you have some more of this. Go on now. Scoot." She gave him a small push with her foot.

Tibo leaned over the can. "Smells good. I could eat it myself."

"Belongs to Smith. I only gave him a taste so he would be sure to come back for more. You feed Hunch from the scrap bag."

She took the empty milk bucket and her water jug

to the shore and set the covered pail down before going to search for the spring. Smith slipped into the shadows, stalking some invisible prey.

The river, the woods, the sky were as fresh and clean as if they had been to a laundromat. Even the birds seemed to have had their voices rinsed so that their songs were like the sparkling stream of spring water Blue spotted only a few yards ahead.

Blue splashed the cold water on her face and bare arms, shivering with pleasure. She filled her jug and returned to the boat.

There was no sign of Lena Finch. The empty milk pail looked somehow lonely on its strip of wet, gray sand.

Tibo hurried down the gangplank. "I gotta go," he explained, trotting into the woods.

On board, she tore a blank page from the log book, and wrote, "Dear Miss Finch: Thank you for the food. It was very . . ." She pondered. ". . . delectable. Sincerely, Blueberry Lincoln." She added a postscript. "When I come back I'll try to bring you a nice present."

She studied the note. If she ever did return this way, Miss Finch might be dead and buried. She knelt and pulled out a wooden chest under the bunk, raised the lid, and studied the carved figures there. The bluebird was her best, maybe good enough to sell to somebody if she and Tibo needed money before they reached her uncle's place. It was difficult to part with any of her creations: the sleeping squirrel, the chipmunk, the pair of kittens, the tiny mouse with its twine tail.

Holding the chipmunk tenderly, she retraced her steps to the shore and placed the wooden figurine and the note on the milk bucket cover, adding a flat rock for weight against the wind. She turned away and sought out a secluded spot in the woods, hoping Tibo was nowhere near enough to peek.

Finished, she returned to the milk pail, frowning thoughtfully. She took her pencil from her hip pocket, removed the note, and crossed out her name. Smarter not to leave it there in case somebody did come searching. She replaced the note.

"Come on, mates!" she called to Tibo and Smith.

"Whatja doin'?" Tibo asked, coming forward.

"Leaving a little present for Miss Finch."

Tibo studied the chipmunk. "Did you make that?"

She nodded.

"Hey, that's good. Did somebody help you?"

"Of course not." She turned, embarrassed by his praise. "Come on, Smith, blast you! We're shoving off."

Tibo pointed. "He's already on board—sittin' there waitin' for the rest of that cat food. I don't know how he can stand the taste of it."

She flashed him a look. "Did you go and . . ."

Tibo's eyes were dark pools of innocence. "I just happened to dip my finger in it—when I was reachin' into the cupboard for a cup. It sure didn't taste as good as it smelt."

"I should make you eat the whole can!"

Tibo made an exaggerated gagging sound, following her up the gangplank.

A few minutes more, all chores attended to, the *Victory* was on its way. Smith ate another portion of cat food while Hunch squawked, "Damn your hide, get out of here!"

"Who's he talkin' to?"

"Repeating what Pa's always hollering at Smith."

Starting the outboard motor, Blueberry glanced back at the shore. She thought she saw a woman in overalls approach and wave. She could not be sure whether it was real or only a shape of mist but she waved in turn, thinking wistfully of the snug house Miss Finch must have in the woods, kettles and dishes shining.

Tibo seemed to share her thoughts. "It would've been nice to stay there and maybe we could have lived with that lady. Only, I guess she don't like kids, especially boys. Not kids like me, anyhow."

"There you go again, feeling sorry for yourself."

"Who else is gonna?" He looked at the sky. "It ain't stormy at all now. The sky's all red where the sun's comin' up."

"Red sky at morning, sailors take warning," Blue recited. "Red sky at night, sailor's delight."

"It looks kind of like a forest fire, don't it? I was in a real forest fire oncet—once—when I was little. Everything got burned up. Exceptin' me. They carried me out but I was chokin' to death from the smoke."

"They who?"

"I dunno. That's when my folks were kilt." He changed the subject. "Hey, look at that old kingfisher swoop down and catch himself a fish! When're we gonna catch one to fry?"

"Pretty soon. I want to put a little distance behind us first, just in case."

"You mean she might go and tell about us?"

"I don't really think so—but you never know." The river was no longer murky. It looked cleaner, clearer, than back home. Perhaps a big, lonesome walleye pike was just waiting for a nice chunk of breakfast on a hook. Smith would purr over some fresh fish. "You get the rods," she told Tibo. "I'll fix one up for you and one for me. I can troll while I steer."

"Troll? I ain't ever fished from a boat before."

"It just means you let your line and bait trail out behind the boat and it moves along with the boat. Are you sure you know how to handle a rod and reel?"

"Sure," he said, but he avoided her gaze. "Although at the Home we mostly fish with poles. I've watched Mr. Bert cast from shore with his rod, though, and it looks easy."

"If you lose your rod overboard I'll sandpaper your eyeballs." It was the grisliest punishment she could think of.

A short time later, she and Tibo sat trolling artificial lures in the wake of the slowly moving craft.

"Keep the reel's brake on," she instructed Tibo, "or else hold your thumb tight against the line so you don't let it spool out. Trolling is easy; it's casting that takes practice."

Tibo nodded, watching his line, his shoulders tense.

"You don't have enough line out yet. Feed it out a bit more—slow and easy."

"Aye, aye, sir." He moistened his lips, hands clamped around the rod. "Why ain't they bitin'?"

"Fishing takes patience, like a lot of other things."

"Yeah, but they ought to be hungry, this early."

Blueberry gave him a sly glance. "Maybe there's a big, starving pike down there named Tibo."

"There ain't any fish called Tibo!"

"I guess not. If there were it would be the size of a minnow. Like you." When Blue was little, Tad had teasingly called her "Miss Minnow."

He flashed a hot look at her. "I ain't no minnow. Hey!" he gasped. "Somethin' struck at my hook!"

Sure enough. Tibo's line went taut.

"Give him some line—play him. But at the same time keep it tight or he'll throw the hook."

Tibo's reel spun crazily, the line racing out.

"Crank the reel back toward you, damn it!"

"I can't—I can't stop it!" The shaking rod in one hand, he fumbled at the spinning handles with the other.

Blueberry lunged forward and wrested the pole from him. She reeled the slack line in swiftly, felt the weight at the lure end, held steady, then gave the rod a backward yank that set the hook firmly. A big fish, right! She reeled the line in, feeling the thrill of a good catch fighting the hook.

"Get the dip net, Tibo—right on the cabin wall. Port side."

He found the net and hurried back at the exact instant she drew the fish to the side of the boat.

Blue seized the net, reached down, and trapped the fish in its heavy mesh. She hauled it up over the side and lowered it against the boards.

"Wow!" Tibo exclaimed, staring at the fat walleye flopping at his feet. "He's a whopper. I never caught one that big before!"

"*You* caught! If I hadn't stepped in he'd have been a mile away from here by now telling his grandchildren about his escape."

"He didn't bite *your* hook. I could've pulled him in by myself. You stole him from me!"

"More likely he'd have pulled *you* in." She gazed at the catch with pride and satisfaction. A fine meal for all.

Tibo yelled, "Look out—you're headin' right toward the bank!"

Blueberry reached for the tiller and swung it quickly. The boat changed course so swiftly that Tibo slid halfway across his seat, and Blueberry fell off balance.

Tibo's grin was malicious, mocking, "You ain't always so perfect either!"

"Shut up. It's nothing to grin about. Why didn't you

grab the tiller yourself when you saw I was busy with this pike?"

"'Cause you don't think nobody can do anything except yourself, that's why."

The words stung because of the truth in them. And she *had* interfered with his catch. Even so, he had no right to grin over their near-accident. He had a sickening kind of grin, she decided. In fact, everything about him was almost more than she could stand. And there was Smith nibbling at a flea on his tail as if he hadn't a care in the world. Old Hunch was unconcerned, too, pecking away at the remains of an oyster shell wedged between the bars of his cage.

A fine crew she had! It would be a miracle if they ever reached Minneapolis.

"All right," she said finally, sullen. "Take your puny little fish and clean it, since you claim you caught it. I don't want to waste my time arguing about it. The scaler and knife are in the tackle box. And don't cut your fingers off."

"It ain't a puny fish." He leaned down and picked up the dip net gingerly, eyeing the still flopping pike, then carried it into the cabin.

Blueberry concentrated on navigating, pretending to ignore Tibo but glancing at him frequently from the corner of her eye. She saw him remove the hunting knife and stand looking down at the gasping fish.

"What're you waiting for?" she called out finally.

"I'm waitin' for him to die. He's still breathin'."

"Well, hit it in the head. Give him a wallop with the blunt end of the hatchet."

"What hatchet?"

"Right in front of you—on that wall hook."

He took the hatchet down, then busied himself getting out the scaler. Again, he hesitated, the fish still making feeble flops at his feet. Suddenly, he pressed his hand to his stomach and made a gurgling noise. He dropped the hatchet and rushed out, leaned over the side and threw up. Finished, he turned toward her, shamefaced. "I can't hit him when he's still breathin'!" He wiped his wet chin with the back of his hand.

Blueberry sighed between her teeth. "Okay. Come here and take over the tiller."

In the galley, she reflected that on top of all the rest of Tibo's faults he was lily-livered. The liver was a most important organ in the body and it took up a lot of space. It would be horrible to go around being lily-livered like Tibo. She reached for the hatchet.

The pike's pink gills still worked faintly. The fish was surely a fighter for life, she thought with grudging admiration. She busied herself taking a cutting board from its niche, fussing with the tackle box, removing a long-dead worm from a hook. Tad would have bawled her out plenty if he found anything like that. She glanced over her shoulder at the pike. Motionless at last. Still. Stone dead.

Her back to Tibo she made a whacking noise on the

cleaning board with the hatchet. "There!" she announced, "That sent him to fish heaven."

Blue carried the pike out to the side of the boat and proceeded to send fish scales shining through the air. Then she gutted it.

"Did it hurt him much when you whacked him?" Tibo's voice held a note of awe, but was also strangely muffled.

"What could hurt more than gasping for breath, or having a hook in your mouth, though they say fish don't feel much."

"Is there a fish heaven?"

"Why not? There's one for cats; has to be."

Tibo stared down at the water. "I'm going to hell."

"What makes you say such a thing?"

"That's what lotsa people have told me. I'm no good. You don't think so either."

She studied him and saw that he was keeping his face averted, head down. "You're not keeping an eye on the river."

"I am so!" He raised his head and she saw the tear stains on his dusky cheeks. "You're just like all the rest of 'em; just because you're bigger you think you kin kick me around and make fun of me! You're a regular bully, like Kelley. You even made fun of the fish I almost caught. I would have got it too but you wouldn't give me half a chance." His face worked.

She felt remorse. "I'm sorry, Tibo—cussing at people is a bad habit I have. You're right about the fish. You'd have caught it by yourself, probably." A lie. He would have lost the pike sure as anything. "I got excited and butted in. You're doing real well, Tibo. Honest. Now I'm going to fry your fish and we'll all have a nice, hot breakfast. You keep steering the boat. You're getting to be an expert at it."

"I ain't hungry," he murmured.

She went into the galley. "Maybe you can force yourself to eat a little of it once you smell it frying." She paused. "It's nicer when shipmates eat together. We'll anchor and just enjoy ourselves, okay?"

He shrugged.

The one thing Ma conceded Blue was very good at was frying fish. Heat some oil in a pan, sprinkle with flour, salt and pepper—and slice some onion to have on the side. There was nothing more beautiful than onions; round white flowers wrapped up in themselves.

With the fish sizzling in a pan, almost done, she called Tibo.

"I put out a plate for you, mate. Shall I shut off the outboard—or can you do it?"

"I kin do it. I watched you."

She waited. The engine died. "Fine, Tibo." She lowered the anchor. "Now, I'll put some food on your plate, if you want."

"I don't care," he said with false indifference. "I guess I feel a little hungrier now."

In a minute, they sat in the stern hunched over their tin plates. Smith bowed over his own dish, looking as reverent as a preacher.

"More?" Blueberry questioned when Tibo had quickly cleaned his plate.

"I guess I kin force down a little more." He hesitated. "You cooked it real good."

"It would take a mighty bad cook to spoil a fat, big fish like that one." She gazed out at the shoreline. Arrow-straight pine trees mirrored themselves in the water. She wondered again if Uncle Stewart would have servants. If not, she could cook for him. Unless he had a wife. Maybe he had children. Maybe a girl her own age. What if she and her cousin didn't get along?

Tibo whispered, "Hey, look at Smith."

She did. Smith was inspecting his sandbox. He walked around it warily, dipped a paw in, then with an air of decision stepped into the box and squatted.

Blue grinned triumphantly at Tibo.

"First cat I ever knowed that had a private privy," Tibo commented and giggled. He immediately sobered. "Whatja want me to do now, Blue?"

"You can take it easy for awhile; we'll clean dishes when we make port tonight. Time to haul anchor now and be on our way again. Maybe reach or be on the Little Skunk by dark. That'll be a good lap of our journey behind us."

Except for a faint grayish light behind the western clouds there was no sunset radiance when the *Victory* reached the Little Skunk River. A spatter of hail racketed against the cabin, then subsided. The gusty wind was heavy with moisture, promising a downpour.

"Wow," Tibo said, "the Skunk's really a big river—twice as big as the Chicksaw."

"It broadens still more where it flows into and through White Wing Lake. You can see the lake way in the distance." It was pouty looking, and she did not like the froth on the steel-colored waves. "I don't want to be crossing that big lake in the dark. Soon's we see a likely harbor we'll head toward it." She increased the speed of the motor but the *Victory* made little progress against the strong headwind. In the far distance, a water skier skimmed along the surface, then receded from view.

Tibo turned the collar of his jacket up. "Is the Mississippi even bigger'n this?"

"Lots."

"And where's that big city we're goin' to?"

"Minneapolis. It's on the Mississippi, across from St. Paul. Right now I'm going to steer in behind that point ahead and see if there's a handy beach for the night. You be ready for action."

As they rounded the point, she studied the shoreline. "Looks good." Another point extended out from a kind of cove to provide a windbreak. Blueberry shut off the motor, tilted the propeller blades above the water, and let the current drift the boat slowly shoreward.

Smith was on the prow, eager to leap to freedom.

Paddling the boat closer to land, Blue reminded him, "I'm trusting you, Smith."

Their temporary haven was wilder and scraggier than back at the Finch place. The wind had a biting edge to it. And there had been enough rain the night before to make the ground soggy, the fallen wood damp.

"If you have to go, Tibo, you'd better hurry. Those rain clouds are going to burst open soon. We'll have to cook supper on board." Smith had already disappeared into the woods.

Tibo jumped onto the sand beside Blue. He started forward, then hesitated as something stirred in the underbrush. "Maybe that was a wolf—or a bear."

"Most of the wolves have been hunted to death. Maybe just a big porcupine. Porkies won't hurt you if you leave them alone. You have to learn not to be lily-livered."

He looked at her blankly, then trudged toward the trees. Tad's jacket flopped near his knees making him look like a small clown. Funny thing, he didn't even know how ridiculous he looked. Funnier yet, she imagined how she would fight anybody who dared to laugh at him.

She stretched and inhaled the spice fragrance of pine needles and rotted leaf mold. A crane flew up from a marshy spot, its wings working like wide, blue sails. From the direction of White Wing Lake a loon called, the sound a kind of black silver cutting through the silence.

There was a crackling again in the bushes nearby. Apprehension brushed *her* now. A stray cat? Possibly even a female. She looked around for Smith but he was nowhere to be seen.

She buttoned her jacket. "Kind of scarey here, but nice," she whispered, feeling that Tad stood right beside her. "Pretty soon I'll light the lantern and after super maybe I can teach Tibo how to play cribbage."

Tibo reappeared. "It's sure lonesome around here."

"Did you see Smith?"

"Yeah. He was crawlin' along on his belly, huntin'."

"A yummy field mouse steak, probably."

"I seen the porky too." He stretched his arms out. "He had quills this long! He seen me and he left."

Rain struck her face. "You hurry on board. I'll be there in a minute."

She took her own turn in the woods, then whistled for Smith. Only a sleepy-sounding wood thrush answered. Smith could have shore leave for a while longer. He would come back soon enough, especially if he did not catch any supper for himself.

In the cabin, Hunch was singing in his cracked voice, "Yankee Doodle, keep it tup, keep it tup. . . ."

"And with the girls be handy," Blue sang the finish. "You couldn't carry a tune in a bucket," Ma had told her. "If you feel like singing, go away where I don't have to listen."

She had been able to sing pretty well along with Tad's harmonica, she reflected. Perhaps she should start practicing on the instrument, herself, tonight.

She turned from the kerosene stove to see Tibo in the stern whittling at a piece of wood he had picked up on shore. He was using the hunting knife.

"You put that knife back where it belongs!" Blueberry ordered. "What d'you think you're doing?"

"I'm tryin' to make a chipmunk, like the one you did."

"What you'll do is cut a finger off."

He looked at her ruefully, returned the knife to the tackle box, then retreated and hurled the crude carving overboard.

"I didn't mean you had to throw it away," she said, sorry.

"It wasn't no good, anyhow."

At cloudy, wind-whipped midnight, Smith had not yet returned. Blueberry stared, sleepless, into the cabin's dimness. Could he have been caught in a hunter's trap? Too smart for that, she argued with herself. And even if there were a female cat around he wouldn't go off with her, especially not in a storm.

He'll be back by morning, she thought. Or any minute now he would jump onto the bunk and curl up at her feet.

In the berth above, Tibo gurgled and snored. Blue curled one arm around her head to shut out that sound and the splash and hiss of the storm, while she tried to ward off thoughts of a trapped or tree-crushed Smith.

Search at Dawn

AT DAWN, THERE WAS AN OMINOUS dark red gleam behind clouds that were twined like huge, hairy ropes on the eastern horizon. Blueberry studied the sky from shore. The unnatural redness was a sign of more bad weather, like an angry boil near bursting. Right now the air was still. Everything seemed to be holding its breath.

She made her way deeper into the woods and called out again as she had been doing for almost an hour. "Smith! Where are you, Smith? Damnation, I'm going to get mad in a minute and give you a thrashing! There's still some canned cat food left. John Joseph Jeremiah Smith—do you hear me?"

A red squirrel scolded from a tree limb; that was all.

Blue went on. Again she visualized Smith caught in the bloody jaws of a trap. She had seen a small fox in a trap once, and she could not forget its frantic eyes.

Her throat felt almost too dry to produce a whistle. Her cheeks and neck stung where springy branches had lashed at her.

Plunging on, she coaxed, "Smith, honey. Next time we catch a fish I'll give the whole thing to you. And when we get to Uncle Stewart's you'll have a big can of wonderful cat food every day, just like the cats on TV."

She kept on for another half hour, then began a wide, searching circle back toward the *Victory*. Her steps lagged even though it was high time the boat was on its way. She had posted Tibo to stand watch by the shore, afraid that if he wandered too far into the woods he might become lost.

Still calling, coaxing, she approached the shoreline. The *Victory* was visible now through the trees and she saw for the first time that the fresh letters she had painted on the prow were beginning to flake off. The original name, *Mud Hen*, was starting to show through.

She bit her lip. She might have known that any paint Pa stored around would be no good. Or else this was a punishment for her having stolen it. The flaking

Victory letters seemed an evil omen, like the glowering sky.

"Oh, Smith, sweetie—we have to shove off!"

A crow yelled from the topmost branch of a birch tree. "Caw. Haw-haw!"

She picked up a pebble and hurled it at the bird. As she walked on, an upthrust tree root tripped her. She kicked at it viciously, striking her big toe so hard the pain brought tears to her eyes.

"Fool, dumbbell root!" she muttered.

Tibo called something as she approached.

She ran forward, hope leaping. "Is Smith here?"

"No, but I seen a boat off toward the lake. Maybe somebody's lookin' for us."

"Which way did they go?"

"The other way. I don't think they seen us."

"Just the same, we'd better clear out of here. They're probably heading home somewhere before the storm hits. Let's go."

Tibo stared at her. "Without Smith?"

She cleared her throat and managed a stiff shrug. "That seems to be the way he wants it. It isn't as if it's the first time somebody's run out on me." Tad. Even her dad, going and getting killed. And now Smith. Deserters all! Bitterness was a taste in her mouth. Suddenly, she spat. What was the matter with her! Tad had to leave. And her father hadn't planned to die. Smith must have his reasons too; cat-reasons, anyhow.

With Tibo's help she launched the boat, certain that

Smith would come sauntering forward at the last possible moment.

Far off there was a growl of thunder, a lightning flash.

"Haul in the tow rope," she commanded in a choked voice.

"I already did."

"Then get busy at something else. Go peel a potato to have with the salt pork." She turned so he could not see her tears.

Wiping her face with her sleeve, she started the engine and steered toward open water. Tibo, she saw, was clumsily working at the potato with a peeler. As she watched, he stuffed a slice of the raw vegetable into his mouth.

Blueberry started to yell at him, then stopped herself. Maybe she had been yelling and cursing everybody too much, especially Tibo. It wasn't fair to take out her hurt on him.

Lightning crashed into the pines. She gave the outboard full throttle, racing against the storm. One of three islands loomed far off in the lake ahead. If the weather became too rough they could work toward the nearest island, haul in there, and sit out the blow.

The prow where Smith so often sat was empty. He's only a cat, she told herself. There were a million cats in the world.

It did not help. She wondered if anything ever would.

The daytime sky was dark except for lightning flashes. The hot wind had become a gale. The lake surface was studded with hammering raindrops. Rain poured from Blue's long hair as she sat at the tiller. The potatoes and salt pork she had eaten felt like a sodden weight in her stomach. Because of the dark sky and rain, the compass in her hand was scarcely visible. The largest of the three islands had been straight south and if she read the compass correctly they were heading toward its western side. She thought she could make out the island's vague bulk ahead.

Spray kicked over the prow as she directed the *Victory* into the wind, striving to keep the boat going straight into the waves. A sideslap from one of those foaming waves could capsize even so sturdy a boat as hers and Tad's.

"It's really comin' in over the sides now!" Tibo called from the bow where he was using a tin can to bail out the water.

The tarpaulin covering the stern opening of the cabin was all but useless, flung every which way by the wind. Beyond the whipping canvas she saw Tibo struggling valiantly, almost ankle deep in water.

"Keep at it, mate—you're doing fine!" she yelled back. "All we have to do is reach the island."

There was a strangely sloppy feeling to the tiller. The rudder had been broken when she and Tad took over the boat and he had repaired it with two stout bolts. However, he had always planned to have the piece welded when he had enough money to hire it done.

The *Victory* was not holding the course she had set for it. Alarmed, she swung the tiller in an attempt to compensate for the boat's leftward drift. There was a brittle, snapping noise. A piece of jagged metal spun briefly to the surface before it plunged out of sight. The rudder! Completely severed!

Blue let go of the useless tiller, staggered forward, and seized an oar from the cabin. Back in the stern she thrust the oar blade into the water, trying to substitute it for the missing rudder.

"Tibo—get the life preservers!" she cried above the storm. "Hurry! Remember, pull it over your head the way I showed you. Then bring me mine!"

Tibo stood up, his eyes huge. "Are we gonna drown?"

"Of course not—but safety first. Only, don't just stand there!"

The strong current of the river flowing through the lake gripped the *Victory*, helping to carry it generally on course, but at each second the opposite sweep of the wind-pushed waves threatened to turn the craft broadside. Blueberry's oar felt like a straw against the contending forces.

Tibo groped his way to the cabin. He stretched toward an overhead compartment.

"I can't reach them. I ain't tall enough!"

"Then grow! Jump! Climb up on something!" She dared not leave the stern, feeble though the oar-rudder was.

Tibo fell back, leaped again, then caught hold of some projection and clawed a way upward. One life jacket plopped to the cabin floor. Another.

Tibo came toward her, dragging both jackets.

The boat swerved and tipped to one side. With all her strength, Blue worked with the oar. The boat steadied, clung to its course, and plunged on.

"Put it on!" Blue yelled.

"I'm tryin' to!"

The life jacket was too large, its orange bulk reached below Tibo's knees. Would it be more a hindrance than a help? She ground her teeth and worked the oar.

"I can't tie things very good," Tibo admitted, fumbling with the fastening strings.

"Do the best you can. Now hand me mine."

He pushed the other life jacket at her.

Blueberry waited until a moment when the boat seemed stable, then pulled the preserver over her head. She tried to tie the fastening tapes with one hand and almost lost her grip on the oar. "Tibo—crawl closer and try to tie my strings too. I can't manage alone."

With fierce determination the small fingers worked over the ties on her jacket.

"Good thing I brought you along," she said. She

strained to see ahead. The large island was definitely before them now, nearer than she expected. Too near. She sucked in her breath, glimpsing shoreline rocks and the gnarled roots and weather-twisted branches caught there. They seemed poised to claw at the *Victory*.

With false calm, she instructed, "Whatever happens, Tibo, stick with the boat. As long as it stays afloat, you hang on and float with it."

"Aye." His own voice was made of wood that seemed to splinter. "Uh, you'll be hangin' on right beside me, won't you, Blue?"

"Right. We stick together. Main thing is to keep our heads. Don't panic. Getting panicky is. . . ."

A large, cylindrical object scraped against the hull, skidded toward the stern. There was a dull crack.

"Hang on!" she cried. The boat dipped and swayed, bucking like a tormented horse toward the treacherous shore.

Blue slid from the stern seat.

Suddenly, it seemed that the island itself was rushing toward them. The rocks and driftwood reared up like an enormous, grayish-green monster, claws outstretched.

The *Victory* scraped bottom, shuddered, then bucked again. There was a boom as if a mammoth fist had struck. Blue went spinning backward, hands clutching at the wind.

She lay dazed, blood dripping. She pressed her

palm to her forehead, then lowered it and look blankly at the bright redness. There had been no pain. The boat was still, like something dead.

"Tibo!" she called.

There was a gagging sound. She saw him hanging over the boat's side, throwing up.

In her relief, she exclaimed, "It's the raw potato slice that did it!"

He swung his pale face toward her, then was sick again.

Blueberry swayed to her feet, fighting for balance. She tried to survey the chaos. The *Victory* was partially on its side. In the cabin, supplies and gear had tumbled from their places; doors hung open. Pans and utensils lay scattered. Even the box of whittled figurines had slid out from below the bunk and tilted over. She saw the wooden bluebird, one delicate wing broken.

Tibo looked around slowly. His gaze fixed on Blueberry. "You're bleedin'!"

"I know. Are you all right?"

"I guess. Anyhow, we ain't drowned yet."

"We can't very well drown when we're stuck right on land. The boat's hurt bad, though."

"You kin fix it up, can't you?"

"With what?" At the alarm in his eyes, she added, "I don't know. We'll see." She made her way to the cabin to try to find the first aid kit. Smith was the smart one! Maybe he had an—an intuition, that was the word. Animals were said to sense things sometimes that humans couldn't.

She found a roll of gauze and wrapped it around her head. Tad's shaving mirror showed that the wound was not deep but it bled a lot. She had always been a good bleeder. Once it was something to brag about, but she did not feel like bragging about anything now.

Tibo ventured to a standing position, looking at the island. "There ain't any sign of anybody livin' here. But there might be, like back at Miss Finch's cove."

Blueberry stood beside him, bracing herself against the slant of the boat. "No, it looks plain wild. Who would build on an island like this out in the middle of a big lake?"

Tibo shivered although the wind was not cold. "Yeah. Looks like a jungle."

"Even if I could patch up the boat," she mused, "there's no way to steer it now." She studied the island again. "There's nothing to do but stay here until we can figure out something else to do." To reassure him and herself, she added, "It won't be so bad, if there's a nice brook to drink from. We can fish and—well, then, somebody will come along and rescue us. There have to be people over on the mainland."

"There was that boat I seen."

It could have come from a long way off, she thought. The mainland, wherever it was, was invisible in the driving rain.

Blue tossed off her life jacket. "Standing here

talking isn't going to help anything." She lowered herself over the side.

The *Victory* lay half-in and half-out of the water. The foremost rock, sharp-edged as a knife, had ripped a long gash in one side. Fortunately, the side was tilted above water level so that no water was flowing in. On the other side a crooked snag gripped the bow in a hook-like clutch. That could be remedied with the hatchet. But without timber or caulking compound, how could she seal the gap?

There was a croaking sound from within the cabin. Hunch!

Blue scrambled back up over the side. There was the parrot, his cage sagging at a crooked angle from its hook so that he staggered drunkenly to keep upright.

"Onward and upward!" he yelled senselessly.

She winced. How would they ever reach Minneapolis now? Even if somebody did rescue them, there were only two dollars in the money belt she wore. Two dollars wouldn't even buy bus tickets back to Chicksaw Landing.

She took the cage off the boat, and set it on the shore.

Tibo followed, still wearing the life jacket.

"Take that off," Blueberry commanded.

"Yes'm."

"That isn't sailor language."

He looked from her to the stranded boat. "We ain't sailors no more."

"You don't have to rub it in." Captain of a wrecked boat, that's what she was. She walked off into the rain. She had not only wrecked the boat but everything else. Without the *Mud Hen*. . . . The *Mud Hen!* The blow on her head must have been worse than she thought.

She took a deep breath and walked back to Tibo. "First thing we have to do is build some kind of shelter. With the help of the kerosene we'll start a fire. Then we'll have a good hot meal of some kind. And then—well, we'll carry everything ashore that we'll need. Next, when the weather clears, I'll start working on the boat."

"You said you wouldn't be able to steer it."

"I'll figure out something." Her chin firmed. "I didn't start out on this trip to spend my life on a deserted island!"

Storm Refuge

BLUEBERRY AND TIBO HUDDLED CLOSE together under the wind-shaken canopy created from the tarpaulin that had been on board. All day and now at night the storm continued.

"The water's risin' fast, ain't it," Tibo said, staring out into the gloom. The *Victory* was barely visible. "What if the water reaches the hole in the boat's side?"

"So far, it can't because the *Victory* rises with the water, but it can only float so high because of that big snag holding it fast."

She had hacked at the snag briefly but there had been little time to spare. The tarpaulin shelter, crude though it was, had taken a long while to construct against the whipping rain and wind. Using spare ropes and lines from the boat, she had managed to stake the ropes like guy lines so that the tarp provided a roof and sloping windbreak. At the open end of the shelter she had thrust sharpened branches into the rain-softened soil, then interlaced them with pine boughs as an extra wind screen. It helped, but nothing could keep the rain from leaking down on the pair of them.

Tibo sat hunched in a damp blanket, pressed close to Blue. "Maybe it'll rain forever. Like in the Bible."

"What do you know about the Bible?"

"They teach us about it in Sunday school. Boy! If you so much as whisper you get whacked. There's a picture of old Noah and the ark." Tibo scratched at a bite on his wrist. "All them animals he took along—I wish he hadn't taken any mosquitoes."

"Yeah. The wet weather's making them worse, and the fire's not much help. I'd put some damp grass or leaves on it to make a smudge but then we'd be even chillier than we are."

"The best thing about Sundays," Tibo said, a hint of wistfulness in his voice, "was we sometimes got a dish of pudding at chow time. And once we even had ice cream. The man at the store in town gave it to us because his freezer went out of whack and it was startin' to melt."

"That was Mr. Lund," Blueberry said. "He gave me some candy once after there was a fire. It tasted smokey but I ate it anyhow." She sighed, drawing her own blanket closer around her shoulders. "Someday I'm going to buy a whole box of chocolate-covered cherries and eat it all by myself."

"I wonder what they had to eat at the Home tonight."

She glanced at him suspiciously. "Do you wish you were back there?"

"Heck no. Only—I guess most of our grub got soaked, didn't it?"

"Yes," she said in a flat voice.

Hunch, his cage swinging from a nearby branch, a scrap of oilcloth over the roof, squawked something in a language only another parrot could understand. Maybe it was parrot-swearing. He had not much cared for the soggy food she had managed to provide for him. Her dream of making pan bread had vanished; the flour sack was a sodden mash of dough. There was very little undamaged food left. Some beef jerky in a jar, one can of milk, canned beans, a can of soup . . . and the remains of the canned cat food that she had never had a chance to give to Smith.

She stood abruptly to stop the thought of him. "I'm going to crawl out and add some wood to the fire."

The fire and extra firewood were protected from the worst of the downpour by the overhanging branches of a large maple. And with the help of the wide board she had used as a gangplank she had created a reflecting wall to send the warmth of the fire into the shelter, remembering the various tricks Tad had taught her about such things.

The board was not much of a success, she thought ruefully. But creating a fire at all had been an achievement, even with liberal squirts from the kerosene can before lighting. The fuel supply was diminishing swiftly, but there was no point in saving it since the kerosene stove was at such a tipsy angle it was useless.

She placed several carefully chosen chunks of wood onto the fire, then crawled back under the tarp. She tried to summon some brightness to her voice. "I wouldn't be a bit surprised but what the sun will be shining in the morning. Then we can dry things out and get a better look around."

"You said earlier that the sun might come out by sunset."

"It's important to keep hoping, to look on the bright side of things."

"Hopin' for things never did me any good. I used to hope somebody rich would come along and 'dopt me. But I don't have no rich kinfolk like you got. Your uncle, I mean." The firelight burnished his eyes. "Have you really got a rich uncle, Blue?"

There was a snap in her voice. "You don't think I'd make something like that up, do you? I can't swear to how rich he is but he's right there in Minneapolis. He sends me wonderful presents at Christmas time." She changed the subject. "Tomorrow we should be able to see across to the mainland. There has to be somebody living there. If we don't see them, maybe they'll see us."

"You said maybe they'd be able to see our fire and would come rescue us before now."

"Don't keep telling me what I said. Who's going to be out scouting for anybody in a storm like this? I'm going to go to sleep. Then in the morning, rain or shine, I'll start chopping the *Victory* free—and hope water doesn't start to pour into her during the night. You stretch out too, Tibo. We can share the two blankets."

"Sometimes at the Home three of us had to sleep together. It's warmer that way, though." He stretched out beside her.

She curled herself together, seeking warmth. "I wish you'd stop harping about the Home. A person would think it was something wonderful."

"It's a helluva lot dryer than this!"

"If you swear around Uncle Stewart he might not try to help you out at all."

"I won't," he promised. "You better watch it, yourself."

She could sense Tibo's smirk even though she could not see it. He was right, of course. She would have to be careful. She had been careful when she had written her letter to Uncle Stew, not telling him too much about herself because there were some pretty bad things, even aside from the cussing. But he had never had a chance to read it, anyhow.

The back section of the dictionary said that the name Stewart meant "keeper of the estate."

Hunch gave a sleepy squawk. If they ran out of food altogether, she would let him out of the cage to try to find food for himself. Only, he had been a prisoner for so many years, including all the years old Molly Mickleson had kept him as her pet before she died. Molly had left a note saying that she was leaving Hunch to Tad for all the chores Tad had done for her without pay. Hunch would not know what to do for himself, let free. Not like Smith.

If Smith were curled beside her now it would be like having a warm, soft stove there. She hoped that wherever he was he was out of the storm, his belly full of wild things he had found to eat.

Once, shortly before morning, she was awakened by Tibo crying out. She turned over and saw him strike blindly at the darkness.

"*Abuelo!*" he called out. "*Abuelo!*"

Blueberry raised herself on one elbow. "You're only dreaming, Tibo. Nothing's going to hurt you. Go back to sleep now."

He gave a small groan, then was silent, again asleep.

Abuelo. An Indian word? She closed her own eyes once more.

When she opened them again, she saw a golden

light casting pale blue morning shadows over her and the world beyond. She leaped up, exclaiming, "The sun's shining, Tibo! I told you it would. Wake up—oh, just look!"

The first rays of the newly risen sun made every leaf, branch, wave, and pebble sparkle as if a vast cargo of jewels had been heaped around; diamonds, mostly, but winking sapphires too where the lake spread its colors, and emeralds caught in all the trees. Even the strands and spokes of tree spiders glistened, like angel's hair on the school Christmas tree.

Blue ran down to the open shore, soaking up the still feeble warmth of the sunlight. There was the *Victory*, the gash in its side still a few inches clear of the water, She sucked in her breath, feeling relief and a nameless joy.

Tibo, hauling at his loose-fitting pants, loped to where she stood. "Hey, there's land way over there! I don't see no sign of houses though."

"There might be some tucked back behind the trees somewhere." She frowned. "It's a lot farther off than I hoped—too far for me to swim. Maybe if we go around to the other side of the island the opposite shore will be closer. And we'll look on the island for a creek or a spring; the jug's just about empty. I should've thought to catch some rain water. Right now I'd better try to find something to eat. You go gather more wood."

After breakfast, they would have to try to catch

some fish, she decided. With fish and fresh water, a person could live a long while. It was too early in the season for berries, but she might be able to find some wild, miner's lettuce or young dandelions for greens.

Back at the shelter, Blueberry boiled damp oatmeal over a refreshed fire, poured on diluted evaporated milk, and used the remains of a jar of molasses for sweetening. Afterward, she and Tibo draped blankets and jackets on bushes to dry, and investigated the stranded boat for a closer check on the safety of the goods still stored there.

The sun was high by the time they set out to explore the island. After a strenuous hike they reached the other side. Although the mainland was nearer than from the western shore, it was barricaded by numerous inlets and backwaters that made a maze of bogs.

"Ugh!" Tibo grunted. "Nobody would build there, for sure. Looks like it could be full of alligators."

"There aren't any alligators in Minnesota."

"Nor tigers or elephants either. I like elephants. I seen 'em on TV. If I don't join the navy maybe I'll learn to be a zoo keeper."

"The way you eat all the time you'd probably steal the peanuts from the elephants."

"They're a lot bigger than I am. It would be fun to be a monkey, swingin' around by the tail."

"You're close enough to one," she said, but she grinned to take any sting out of it.

It was on their return that Tibo spied a creek spilling through a shallow ravine. He raced toward it, and Blue jogged after him. She studied the stream. "Muddy now, from the storm, but it'll clear up later. Only, it might be polluted."

"What d'you mean?"

"You know, dirt and crud from people dumping their garbage and such."

"There ain't nobody here."

"I guess not. The water's probably safe enough." She glimpsed orange color in the distance. "Looks like a pretty flower over there." She went toward it.

Tibo raced ahead. "Some flower!" He kicked the can labeled ORANGE NECTAR. "But it means people must have been here."

"Somebody out fishing, maybe, or stopping to picnic."

"Wish they'd come rowin' over today. Hey, there's something else. It looks like—an arrow!"

It was; imbedded in a rotted stump, its feathered notch still bright though drenched.

"Do you think there could be Indians around here?" Tibo's voice was both hushed and excited.

"There aren't any wild Indians anymore. You're part Indian yourself, some people say."

He did a mock Indian dance, imitating what he imagined was an Indian yell, patting his mouth with the flat of his hand.

"You don't know anything about Indians except

from Western movies. They don't whoop around like that. Miss Holm told us that there are Indian steel workers and lawyers and doctors." She remembered Tibo's nightmare cry. "What does *abuelo* mean? That's what you called out in your sleep last night."

He concentrated. "Uh—it just means 'Grandpa.' I don't remember sayin' it but when I was real little I'd dream there was fire all around and I'd yell that word. It's Spanish, Mr. Bert says. But I dunno. That arrow don't look very old. Where's that gun you said you brought, Blue?"

"On board." She studied the arrow again. "Somebody was target practicing, probably. Come on. I have to see about chopping away the snag from the boat. You go hunt for young dandelion leaves."

"For why?"

"To eat. They're full of vitamins, the teacher says."

Tibo made a face. "I thought we were gonna go fishin' this mornin'."

"That'll now have to wait until later."

Back at the *Victory*, Blueberry rolled her jeans up to her thighs and waded in. She began chopping at the upturned root that imprisoned the boat. The wood was much tougher than she had anticipated. Perspiration trickled down from the matted bandage around her head, and her hair was in a tangle. The comb that had been in her hip pocket had been lost; one thing she had no hope of whittling from wood was a comb.

Tibo returned from his searches with a pan full of

dandelions. Then, on his own, he began to collect fallen wood to drag to the fire site. Blue, resting briefly, decided that he was shaping up pretty well. Thin though he was, he might grow up to be really good looking with those big dark eyes and long lashes. She hoped Uncle Stewart would like him. Perhaps he would adopt them both. No, that was expecting too much.

She chopped steadily, then paused to rest again, and climbed on board. Struggling for balance on the slant boards, she sought out Tad's dictionary which was still safe in her knapsack. She ran a finger along the names in the back pages. There was no "Tibo" listed. But Ma's name, Marge, was there. It meant "a pearl." Blueberry put the book back, checking on the necklace, the perfume bottle, and the harmonica. She removed the instrument. If they were still marooned here tonight she might try playing it. According to the water-stained calendar there would be a moon.

Moonlight and music, she thought with a wry grimace. She remembered Ma sitting once, in the moonlight, alone, holding the almost stringless guitar that had belonged to Blue's father. Ma had just sat there, picking out a little tune on the first string, something sad and lonesome sounding.

Blueberry went back to work with the hatchet, wondering if Ma missed her or if anybody had started searching for her and Tibo. If they looked, they would see that the *Victory* was gone. But they might decide it had broken its moorings and drifted off somewhere. Most likely, they would search in the woods because of her lie about going camping. Even if they did figure out the truth, they wouldn't be expecting to find her here on this island in the middle of White Wing Lake.

The hatchet blade bit into the snag again. The stubborn wood was hanging by a thread. With a final whack she cleaved through. The gnarled claw dropped at the water's edge. But nothing happened. Instead of the *Victory* immediately floating higher, it stayed as it was.

Blue squatted down and for the first time saw the snags holding the underside of the boat.

"Oh, hell!" she exclaimed. Still, what difference would it have made if she had freed the boat entirely? The gap in the hull remained, and the rudder was gone.

Tibo stood on shore, gawking at the sky. "There's a plane up there! Maybe they're lookin' to rescue us."

Blue looked up as the small plane disappeared. "Fat chance." Even as she said it she felt a faint tug of disappointment. Not that she wanted to be discovered. But—well—it would be something if anybody cared enough to send out a real plane. "I'm going to cook those dandelion greens for us," she said. "And there's a bit of salt pork, and some beans, left." She splashed ashore. "Afterwards, we'll have a hot fudge sundae. Joke."

Tibo licked his lips. "I'd rather have butterscotch."

"You can't be fussy," she said. "When I buy that box of chocolates, I'll give you some."

In the afternoon, she tried casting for bass, with no luck. Tibo's casting attempts ended in snarled backlashes so that he gave up and sat brooding, poking a stick at an anthill.

More and more, as the afternoon wore on and sunset colored the sky, Blueberry's gaze went toward the lake and the opposite shore. Once, she thought she saw a rowboat far off. The boat disappeared. At the time the first star peeked out of the twilight blue, there was a distant sound of a motorboat. Otherwise there was nothing but the usual forest rustlings and the voice of a hoot owl tuning up.

Tibo sat sucking on the green stem of a foxhead. "What if nobody ever finds us? We could starve to death. One of the guys at the Home told about how some people that crashed in a plane ran out of food and started to eat each other!"

"You shouldn't listen to such things. Anyhow, you wouldn't have to worry. You're so small you wouldn't make one square meal." She considered what food there was for some kind of supper. There was one potato left, a nearly full can of milk, two or three small pieces of jerky, a few strips of salt pork, and onions.

Tibo helped her build up the fire. When the scant fare was ready, they sat eating, the darkness moving in around them. Far off, a train whistled. Probably some pokey freight train, Blue thought, but the sound was haunting.

"Some day I'm going to take a train and go far, far away." She had been in Brainerd one Saturday with her folks and they had stayed until after dark. On the way home they had seen a train crossing the night-blue land, its rows of windows shining, the headlight on the locomotive stroking back and forth like a huge, white broom. She had glimpsed people sitting at tables in one of the coaches, flowers in glass vases, and waiters in white jackets.

"I had a dream once," Tibo said. "A big train came roarin' right toward me and I just leaped right over it! It was as real as anything."

"A person can do anything in dreams. Sleeping or awake." The moon the calendar had promised was hanging in the sky, casting bright patterns among the trees. She wondered if the flag the first American astronauts had planted was still flying there.

Blueberry drew the mouth organ from her pocket and blew into the instrument's reeds experimentally a few times.

"Whitey at the Home had one of those once," Tibo said. "But then he lost it or somebody stole it. They called him 'Whitey' 'cause his hair was white and his eyelashes was white, but he wasn't any older'n me. His eyes were almost pink."

"That's what they call an albino. Tad had a pet rabbit once that was an albino." She tried to play

"America the Beautiful" on the harmonica but none of the notes came out as they were supposed to. She tried "Home on the Range," and then "The Beer Barrel Polka." It was hopeless. She tapped the instrument against her palm, as she had seen Tad do, and started to put it back in her pocket. "Some people can pick up a mouth organ and play it right off. You have to have an ear for it, I guess."

"Kin I try, Blue?"

She hated to share something of Tad's but Tibo had a begging look. "Well, okay, but don't get it full of spit."

"I won't." He carefully spat, wiped his hands on his pants, and reached out. "I ain't never played one before, and I don't know many songs."

"You can't do worse than I did."

"That's for sure!" he agreed so heartily that Blueberry winced. "I know what I'll try." With only a bit of fumbling he was soon picking out the melody of "Silent Night."

It was a dumb thing to play in the middle of May, Blue thought, but at least she could recognize the tune. The third time around, Tibo scarcely missed any notes.

"I guess you got an ear for it," she said grudgingly, envious. "What other pieces do you know?"

He thought, then launched into "Jesus Wants Me for a Sunbeam."

Blue recognized it vaguely from the few times she

had gone to Sunday school with her friend Donna Schmidt. "Maybe I can teach you some peppier tunes. Like 'The Beer Barrel Polka.' My Ma likes that one." She whistled it, something she did better than singing, and Tibo practiced until he almost had it memorized.

He beamed at her. "I'm gettin' good fast, ain't I?"

"That's for others to say. But maybe you are a natural born musician, like I'm a natural born artist. Now you give that back to me. We have to think about what we're going to do tomorrow. Maybe in the morning I can climb a tall tree and hang a piece of cloth there that somebody will recognize as a distress signal."

Reluctantly, Tibo handed her the harmonica. "I wisht I had one. Kin I play it again tomorrow?"

"I guess so. Only, we have to work hard at fishing. I'll bet Uncle Stew knows how to play the mouth organ."

"If he knows we're comin' and we don't get there, he'll send somebody out lookin' for us, won't he?"

She avoided his gaze. "Sure. Unless he's sick or had an accident. You can never tell about acts of God."

"What's an axe of God?"

"*Acts.* Acts are things that just happen, like hurricanes or chicken pox or getting struck by lightning."

Tibo looked out at the calm, silver-shining lake. "Or like my kinfolk gettin' burnt up in the fire?" He paused. "Are acts of God always bad things?"

She tried to think of something that was not tragic or dreadful. "Well—no. The *Victory*'s being wrecked, that was bad. But the sun shining today, that was a good thing." She started toward the storm shelter. "Those warm, dry blankets are going to be wonderful!"

"Yeah." Tibo followed her, humming the melody of "The Beer Barrel Polka."

When Ma was feeling good, she would sometimes whistle the polka to herself. "Your real pa was a fine dancer," she told Blue once.

Blue tried to picture such dances now as she spread out the dry blankets. For the first time since she had left Chicksaw Landing she felt a strange pang. Whether it was from homesickness or remorse, she did not know but it made the chant of the hoot owl sound even sadder than it usually did.

Harley

Before going to bed that night, Blueberry removed Tad's old shotgun from the boat and carried it toward the shelter. The firing mechanism was broken and she had no ammunition. Still, if some prowler or fleeing criminal threatened her and Tibo, the sight of the gun might make them hesitate. She leaned the gun against a tree next to the dying campfire. A furry shape skimmed through a patch of moonlight. Unreasoning hope flared up before she glimpsed the stripes of a raccoon.

She stretched out beside the already sleeping Tibo. Wherever Smith was, he was not on this island. She tried not to think of him. How good the dry blankets smelled! She inhaled what seemed the yellow fragrance of sunlight caught in them. Could odors have colors? It was her last thought before she fell asleep.

Faint mist hung over the lake when she awoke, stretched, and prepared to face a new day. Combing her hair with her fingers, she started toward the spot where she and Tibo had carried a waterlogged plank that had washed up on shore. They had laid the plank on two convenient tree stumps, put their remaining scraps of food on it, and covered it with a ragged oilcloth which Blueberry tied in place.

The plank-table was concealed by a bramble of wild blackberry bushes. Blue went through a gap in the thorny hedge, then sucked in her breath. The oilcloth had been ripped off. Plates, spoons, and pans lay scattered. On its side lay the oatmeal carton, its soggy remains spilled over pine needles.

Blueberry ran forward. The few scraps of salt pork she had saved, and the partly full can of milk were gone. Even the onions had been strewn around.

The wind? No, wind that strong would have tugged the shelter tarp from its moorings. Something slyer, sneakier than wind had invaded the spot! The ground was still moist enough to hold hers and Tibo's footprints, and other prints as well. For there, all around, were the fingerlike tracks of raccoons.

Blue used up most of her favorite swear words. No wonder people called them bandits! "You low-down, cowardly, conniving, heartless, thieving brutes!" she raged. "If my gun were working I'd pepper you all into kingdom come!"

Still muttering, she searched the area in the hope that the 'coons had dropped some of their loot. She found the milk can, only a dribble of its contents remaining, two slightly nibbled onions, and a dented can of baked beans.

She turned her fury in the direction of the storm shelter and strode toward it, yelling at Tibo, "A big help you are, snoring away! Wake up!"

Blinking, he crawled out from under a blanket. "What's the matter?"

"Everything! You'd better start practicing those hymns of yours because Judgment Day is coming sooner than you thought."

He got to his feet, hair hanging across his eyes. "You're talkin' crazy. What d'you mean?"

"The 'coons stole our last scraps of food, that's what."

His mouth hung open. "You mean there ain't *nothin'?*"

She held out a raccoon-nibbled onion and the can of beans. "Here's your breakfast. The only way we're going to have anything else to eat is to fish for it."

Tibo looked slyly toward Hunch. "If we really start starvin'—"

She stared at him in disbelief. "You want to be a regular cannibal like those people in the airplane crash? Hunch is a friend. I'd as soon eat Smith! I never heard anything so terrible. I'll bet you do have savage Indian blood."

"You said Indians were lawyers and steel workers now."

"Well. . . ." She felt trapped. "Maybe so, but I can hardly bear to look at you anymore, the kind of thoughts you have."

He thrust his underlip out. "I didn't say I was thinkin' anything. *You're* the one who just now mentioned eatin' Smith."

"Oh, be quiet. We'll warm up the beans and then we'll fish. You still-fish for bluegills or perch from the stern of the *Victory*. I'll cast for bass in the reeds."

Tibo was mostly silent as they shared the beans, his expression downcast. He licked his spoon, then went to get his fishpole from where it rested near the shelter. Returning, he said, "I gotta have some worms for bait for sunfishin'. Have we got a shovel?"

"Why would anybody take a shovel on a boat? We'll have to use something else." She looked toward the chopped-off end of the snag where she had tossed it to shore. "Maybe we can sharpen that up to dig with; it's about the right shape."

Tibo stood watching as she whittled the severed end of the snag to a flat point. "I'm good at findin' worms," he said. "I can hear 'em wriggling under the ground."

She started to scoff, then thought better of it. She had already hollered at him once today; it wasn't his fault that the raccoons had run off with their food. She said only, "You must have mighty sharp ears."

"Yeah, I do! I can cock my head to one side, just like a robin does." He demonstrated. "Nothin' wrig-glin' here." He moved off, then paused, cocking his head again. "I think I hear somethin' here, Blue."

He looked so serious that she said nothing but picked up the crude digging tool. She worked at the soil that Tibo had designated, for several minutes. No angleworms.

They tried several other locations with no better luck.

Tibo looked puzzled. "I used to be real good at findin' them. Maybe if we try over there under that fallen tree. I'll go over and listen, first."

Whether he heard anything or not—which Blue strongly doubted—it seemed a likely place, one she would have chosen herself, with or without ears.

She dug. Shortly, fat, juicy angleworms squiggled under the probing stick.

"I told you!" Tibo said. Triumph erased the look of earlier gloom. "I heard 'em even from a distance."

"Um-hum," Blue grunted. "Run and get the bailing can to put them in."

When he returned he began dropping the worms into the can along with handfuls of earth. "Maybe worms wouldn't taste bad. Fried."

Blue gave him a look of disgust. "Better boiled, with ketchup on. You go ahead and bait up." She walked off to cast her bass lure near the reeds close to shore.

It was a good time for fishing, she encouraged herself, the sun riding the horizon, the water calm. Each time she cast she visualized a large bass grabbing the hook.

At the end of an hour, her wrists ached. "Damn fish are on a hunger strike," she muttered, studying the shoreline for some other promising spot. A patch of taller, thicker reeds farther on caught her attention. She picked up her tackle box and saw movement at the far edge of the reeds. Something flashed in the sunlight. She made out the aluminum side of a boat, a figure in the stern.

She started to call out, then closed her mouth. There was no telling what kind of person the stranger might be. Ducking among the shadows of bush and tree, she hurried to where the shotgun stood. Armed with it, she crept back to the water's edge.

Blue stood waiting for the stranger's next move. The few movements she could glimpse through the thick reeds seemed stealthy. Had the stranger been spying on her and Tibo all this while? Or perhaps he was only an innocent fisherman. If it was a "he."

She made up her mind that she could not just stand there forever. Boldly, she called out, "I see you! You might as well show yourself—I've got you covered."

For a second, nothing happened. Then, slowly, an aluminum canoe glided out from the rushes. It floated toward her. A sun-browned boy with blond hair was rhythmically dipping his paddle, looking directly at her.

Blue raised her gun. "What do you want?"

The boy looked startled. "I was only doing a little fishing," he said. "Who are you?"

"I don't give my name right off to strangers."

"Oh." He studied her ragged jeans, the bloody bandage around her head. "My name's Harley. Harley Colter." He waved a hand toward the opposite shore. "I live about a half-mile north over there." He pointed to the gun. "Are you hunting? You shouldn't ever point a gun at anybody like that."

"I know how to handle a gun!" His eyes were very blue, she saw, like the blue of lake water out where it was deepest. He appeared to be a couple of years older than she, perhaps fourteen. And he did not look at all dangerous.

She lowered the weapon. "They call me Blueberry. But my real name's Linda."

"Oh," he said again. "Well, what should I call you?"

"You don't have to call me anything." It sounded more rude than she had intended. "I mean, it doesn't matter." She suddenly saw the fine catch of sunfish lying in the bottom of his canoe.

"Were you here last night?" he was asking. "I was out on our dock with my brother and I thought I saw a campfire over here. That's one reason I headed this way. I come over here sometimes, anyhow. It's nice and private and a good place for archery practice."

"We found an arrow. It must have been yours. If I had a good strong bow I'd send some arrows through the raccoons around here. They stole our food last night."

"They're tricky that way. How did you get here? I mean, where's your boat?"

Tibo came running toward them, shouting, holding a small perch. "I caught one, Blue!" He ground to a halt, seeing the boy in the canoe.

Blue began, "He's my little bro—." The blue eyes rested on her. "He's a little kid I brought with me. The boat's hidden around the bend here. Wrecked."

"Gosh, that's too bad." He sent his canoe skimming forward to where he could take a long look at the wounded *Victory*. Then with a couple of sweeps of his oar, he brought the canoe to shore. He got out and stood looking thoughtfully at the boat, thumbs hooked in the belt of his jeans. "That's rough," he said as Blue and Tibo joined him. "Looks like a good stout boat. What happened?"

Blueberry told him. Then, her gaze fixing on his catch of fat sunfish again, she confessed, "We don't have a scrap of anything left to eat. What the storm didn't take the 'coons did. Uh—would you be willing to trade those fish for something—like a wooden statue I whittled myself?"

He cocked an eyebrow. The color of a corn tassel, she decided. There was a small, white scar on one cheek, shaped like a tiny star. "What kind of statue?"

"Well, there's a mouse with a twine tail, a kitten, a

squirrel—you could take your pick." She could not bring herself to part with the bluebird. Though broken, it could be easily mended.

"There are mice and squirrels and cats running wild all over our place. Anyhow, I'm not very keen on statues."

She felt taken aback by his slightly scornful tone but more important was his mention of cats running wild. "Have you seen a cat with gray and white stripes, a white bib, and beautiful lemon-yellow eyes?"

He thought a moment. "Nope. A couple of pure whites, one gray, and one or two orange ones." He leaned over his canoe and picked up the stringer of fish. "You can have these. We eat so many fish in my family we're starting to grow gills. D'you want me to clean them for you?" His hand moved to the knife that hung from his belt in a leather sheath.

"I've got my own knife, and I can clean fish like nothing," Blue said. She noticed how clean Harley's fingernails were, the whiteness of his socks in dark blue sneakers, the fresh T-shirt, and became painfully aware of her grubby appearance: her snarled hair, wrinkled blouse and jeans. The useless gun still drooped from the crook of her elbow. She laid it down. As Harley removed the fish and laid them on some coarse grass, she murmured, "Thanks. There's enough for you to share if you want to stay."

He glanced at his wristwatch. "I'm overdue as it is. I have to go back and help Dad do some painting. We bought a small resort recently and soon the vacationers are going to pile in." He looked toward the *Victory*. "Where were you heading, anyway?"

"Oh, downstream," she replied, cautious.

"Well, you can't go anywhere in that."

"I don't need anybody to tell me!"

Tibo, breaking his wary silence, said, "Blue's gonna fix it by herself."

"With what?" Harley challenged. "There aren't any boat-building materials on this island, that's for sure."

"Nobody said there was," Blue retorted. Just because he was obviously well-to-do with his expensive-looking watch and shiny canoe didn't mean he had to act as if she and Tibo were dummies. Stupid of her, though, to start shooting sparks at him. She needed his cooperation. "Do you know any way I can get some materials?"

He looked thoughtful again. "Well, there's spare lumber and lots of boat stuff around our place. But. . . ."

"That's all I need. Something to patch up the hole. And a new rudder. Then I'll free the boat from those underwater snags, pull her right side up, and we'll be on our way." She thought of the two carefully hoarded dollars in her money belt. Not that that would pay for much.

"It's going to take more than a few hours to patch up that boat, aside from getting a new rudder," Harley said. "I guess I could round up some materials for you, but what're you going to do in the meantime? I'd better go talk things over with my folks. And especially with Jed—he's my big brother. He's awfully busy right now but. . . ." Again, he left a sentence unfinished. "Right now, I have to get going."

Blueberry felt sudden panic. Here was a boy who could help out and now he was preparing to paddle off without having promised anything definite. "Wait," she appealed. "You'll be paid. I'm on my way to see my uncle down in Minneapolis. He's waiting for me. He lives in a big house, with servants. He'd pay whatever it costs to fix up the *Victory*." Under his level gaze, she faltered. "Or I could work it out, helping around the resort. Tibo could work, too."

"I told you: I have to talk to my folks." He pushed his canoe into floating position and got in.

"You're coming back, aren't you?" Blue pressed. "Or maybe Tibo and I could ride back with you."

Harley studied Tibo. "This canoe's pretty light and tippy. I'll be back. Did you think I'd just go off and forget all about you?"

"Well—I couldn't figure out what you were going to do. You didn't definitely say. I'm used to talking things out and taking action."

"I'm used to *thinking* things out." He paddled off, setting a diagonal course toward a tall cedar across the lake.

"Why wouldn't he take us with him?" Tibo asked.

"Because a canoe is easily turned over and he could tell you're too fidgety to sit still for long." She watched the departing canoe. "If I'd been alone he would have taken me along."

Tibo dug his foot into the sand; there were two toes visible now in the worn sneakers. "You kin just leave me here to die, if that's what you want. Nobody would care, anyhow."

"Oh, Tibo. I didn't mean it that way. I only meant—let's not fuss about it. You gather some fresh kindling while I clean these sunfish. We're shipmates, remember?"

"I guess," he said doubtfully. He held up his tiny perch. "Don't forget my fish!" He added, "Not that it's anywhere near as big as that pike I caught."

She took the perch from him. The catch was less than legal size but she said, "It's bigger than anything I caught."

Tibo looked toward the lake. "Do you really think he'll be back?"

"He said he would. He's not the kind that tells lies, that's easy to see."

Tibo did not argue but there was distrust in his eyes.

At noon there was still no sign of Harley. The sunfish breakfast, hearty though it had seemed at the time, did not stave off a growing post-noon hunger. Blueberry strained to see the opposite shore and the solitary cedar toward which Harley had steered. She could dimly make out what seemed to be a dock and the shadowy forms of rowboats lined up on the sand.

"He's sure takin' a long time to come back," Tibo said.

"He told us he had to work for his father." She sat on a rock, whittling at a piece of driftwood, not trying to create any special figure. Sometimes it was better just to follow the contours of the wood to find out what shape was hidden there.

"Maybe his father's mean and beat him up for being late."

"That's silly," Blue said. "I told you we have to trust people sometimes." But Tibo's fear was not entirely farfetched. Harley had been very careful about promising what he would or could do, saying he had to talk everything over with his folks.

As the afternoon slid slowly past, a new anxiety plagued Blueberry. Possibly Harley's father had rushed off to notify the law authorities and at any moment Constable Bemis, or even someone more important, would show up to force her and Tibo back to Chicksaw Landing.

From his cage, Hunch squawked, "Pass the spuds!"

Hunch had not cared much for the old weed seeds and moldy acorns she had found for him. She had tried one of the acorns herself but it was too bitter to swallow. Lush mushrooms grew in a shadowy place but she dared not taste them for fear they might be poisonous.

Tibo paced restlessly, tossing pebbles into the lake. "He was lyin' to us about coming back, no matter what. How can you tell when somebody is lyin', Blueberry?"

"They can't look you straight in the eyes."

"*I* can!"

"I don't doubt it. Anyhow, there are other ways to tell." She paused. "Listen!"

There was the throb of a motorboat. From an unexpected direction a speedy red craft came into view. The blond boy at the helm was unmistakably Harley Colter.

Abandoning any pretense of self-sufficiency, Blue leaped up, waving, and gave a cheer.

Tibo seemed too stunned to do more than stand with his mouth open before he gave his own whoop.

The motorboat sliced toward them, two wings of spray shooting up from its prow. It slowed, then drifted in to shore near the *Victory*. There was no visible cargo of any kind in the boat; certainly no boat-repair supplies. Nevertheless, Blueberry and Tibo ran to the landing site.

Harley stepped on shore, drawing the boat up onto the sand. "Sorry I couldn't get back sooner but I had to work overtime. Dad had to leave, and Mom, too, before I had a chance to talk to them. But when they got back, just a little while ago. . . ."

"What about lumber and other stuff?" Blue interrupted. She secretly looked for black-and-blue bruises or other signs of a beating. There were none.

"Well. . . ." He seemed to require forever to think out what he was going to say. Blue waited impatiently, noticing that he had put on a new T-shirt even whiter than the one before, but that there were specks of green paint on one knee of his pants. "Well,

I told my folks about your predicament—what I knew of it—and Mom said right away that you couldn't stay here but that I should bring you over to Pinerest. That's the name of our resort. Then talk and figure everything out. There's a spare cabin where you can stay for the night. Or longer."

It seemed Harley could talk quite a string of words when he needed or wanted to. "What about the *Victory?*" Blue reminded him.

"That takes some more talking and thinking. Jed's not home from his boatworks in town yet—he started his own business there. When he does get home, well. . . ." He turned, reached into the boat, and brought out a paper bag. "Mom fixed some sandwiches for you."

Blue resisted grabbing them from him. "Thanks—that was real nice of your mom. Honest, can we stay in a cabin overnight?" She took out a neatly wrapped chicken sandwich from the bag and passed it to Tibo.

Tibo tore the wrapping off and bit away half the sandwich with his small, white teeth. "Wow, this is good!" he managed before he produced a loud belch.

"Sure, you can have the cabin, Linda. It's a spare one." He looked around and saw the makeshift shelter. "Do you want to take some stuff with you, like extra clothes? I guess there isn't much here that anybody would bother to steal, if they did happen to come by."

Gulping down a mouthful of food, Blue retorted, "I've got my valuables! There're the statues—and my jewels. And there's Hunch. I couldn't go off and leave him alone."

Harley's eyebrows drew together. "Hunch?"

"My pet parrot. Over there in the cage." She pointed. "He's smart. He hears something once and he can repeat it right off."

"Yeah?" Harley strolled over to the bird. "Hi, handsome."

"Hi, handsome," Hunch echoed. "Hi. I want a cigar, dammit!"

Harley looked back at Blueberry with a questioning grin.

She twisted her toes inside her sneakers, cheeks flushed. "Hunch had a kind of rough bringing up. I've tried to teach him not to swear but he's so damn—darn—ornery. Uh—I'll start picking up my valuable things as fast as I can so your pa won't be mad if you're late back to work."

"Mad? Heck, I've never seen Dad get mad in my life. Or hardly ever. Mom's the one. She has a temper to match her red hair. Hey, how old are you?"

"Going on thirteen."

"I'm going on fifteen," he bragged.

Tibo proclaimed, "I'm going on nine. I'm still small for my age. When I grow up I'm gonna join the navy and become a captain."

Blueberry thought: by the time they reached the end of the journey, Tibo would be claiming that he was sixteen!

"Come on, Tibo," she urged to prevent any further

outrageous statements. "Help me sort out the things we want to take."

They boarded the *Victory*. In the cabin, Blue took the glass necklace out and put it around her neck. Then she unwrapped the bandage and studied her forehead. The cut was partly healed but her skin was smeared and sticky. She dipped some water out of the lake with a pail, returned to the cabin, and gave her face and arms a quick scrub.

"You wash up some, too," she ordered Tibo. "We want to try to make a good impression on Harley's folks."

"Whatever I do it won't make no difference." Gloomily, he splashed a little water on his face. He then watched her tuck a few extra articles into the knapsack and drape her best jeans and shirt-blouse over one arm. "I ain't got no valuables to take."

"I'm not even taking all of mine. Like the statues. We'll be coming back tomorrow, and, as Harley says, nobody is apt to come sneaking around. Now, you be on your very best behavior with Mr. and Mrs. Colter. Remember to say 'thank you' and 'excuse me' and 'please.' "

"Aye, aye, sir."

Blue sighed. "You only say that on shipboard."

"Yes, ma'am," Tibo replied, looking confused.

"All right, come along then." She gave the cabin and the rest of the boat a lingering glance. Silently, she promised: We'll fix it up as good as new, Tad. And nothing's going to stop me, from now on.

Loon-call Sunset

LARGE THOUGH THE COLTER DINNER table was, it had scarcely room enough to bear all the food placed on it. Blueberry had never seen such a scrumptious feast: steamy mashed potatoes, a gorgeous brown roast, gravy, warm rolls and jam, pickles, tomatoes, creamed corn. She tried not to devour her portions too greedily, and carefully avoided putting her elbows on the table or chewing with her mouth open.

Beside her, Tibo smacked, sucked, and chewed with as many gleeful noises as a small pig at a feeding trough. But he looked quite presentable now in the fresh shirt and jeans Mrs. Colter had found for him.

Blue, also, felt and looked far better, having been given a comb and the luxury of a shower bath. It was dreamlike, still: the cozy bathroom with its lovely scented soap and big, fluffy towels as soft and pink as sunset clouds. There had been a large bottle of some kind of perfume on a shelf and Blue had guiltily dabbed a tiny bit behind each ear. She wore her clean jeans and red-checked blouse. The glass necklace glittered around her neck. It gave her an added sense of confidence but underneath she was uneasy. Even the Colters calling her Linda made her feel somehow dishonest although it was her rightful name.

Mrs. Colter pressed more food upon Blue and Tibo. "From what you've told me, Linda, you two haven't had a full meal since you left the orphanage."

Tibo stopped chewing. "She ain't runnin' away from the orph—."

Blue gave him a meaning kick and he was silent.

"What he means," Blue said, "is that I explained to the staff people about my uncle and all and how he wanted Tibo to come too."

Harley's father frowned. "But weren't they concerned—two youngsters taking off in an old boat?"

"The orphanage people don't care," Blue said airily. "They're relieved when kids leave. Everybody around Chick—around Brush Falls—knows that." She added defensively, "Just because the *Victory* isn't all sparkling doesn't mean it isn't safe."

"Still," Mr. Colter said, "somebody in authority

should be notified, especially as you haven't been able to reach your uncle by phone."

"He travels a lot." Blue kept her eyes on her plate. At the Colters' insistence she had twiçe pretended to dial a Minneapolis number on the telephone in an adjoining room that served as the resort office.

Mr. Colter, his eyes as blue as Harley's, looked closely at Blue. "You don't have any relatives in Brush Falls?"

"Nope. They were burned in an awful fire."

Tibo, mouth full, exclaimed, "It's *my* folks that was kilt in the fire."

Blue asserted, "Well, it was the same big fire."

The Colters murmured words of sympathy and then, seeming to feel that the subject was too painful, talked of other things.

Harley sat across from Blue, his brother beside him. Jed had his mother's red hair, and his eyes were light brown like hers. He was heavily built, almost fat. Blue liked his easy smile.

"Jed," his father asked. "Now that you've had a chance to go look at Linda's boat, what do you think?"

"It can be fixed but it'll take awhile, working in my spare time."

"What spare time?" his mother challenged. "You scarcely have time to sleep, working in town all day at your boatworks."

Harley put in, "I can work on the *Victory* after school, and on some weekends."

Blueberry tried to conceal her dismay. She couldn't

wait around for days or weeks! If searchers found her and Tibo and dragged them back, the boat a wreck, she would never be able to hold up her head again.

"Speaking of school," Mrs. Colter addressed Blue, "there must have been some kind of school at the orphanage. You shouldn't be missing so many days of education."

"Oh, we'll be starting school right away in the city," Blue assured her. "One reason why we're in such a hurry. With the right materials Tibo and I can work on the boat ourselves. It would go a lot faster that way."

There was a squawk from Hunch who had been sitting silently on a spare end table. Blue squirmed, fearful of what he might decide to say.

The office phone rang. Harley answered it, then returned. "It's for you, Jed. Rog Cook."

"Boy!" Jed exclaimed, hurrying out. "He could be a mighty important customer."

"I do hope it turns out that way," Mrs. Colter said and passed a plate of brownies. Although they looked delicious, Blue found her appetite suddenly gone. Her stomach churned as she tried to think of some way to start the *Victory* on its journey, and soon. This must be Friday, she calculated. She looked across at Harley.

"Were you skipping school today?"

"No. Teacher's convention in Minneapolis. It's only a couple of hours drive from here. Three days, probably, for a slow boat like the *Victory*."

Tibo protested, "The *Victory* can go real fast!" He reached for another brownie.

"Then we can work all day on the boat tomorrow, Saturday!" Blue exclaimed.

"Can't," Harley said, apologetic. "I've a bagger's job at the store in town. Anyhow, fixing your boat'll take a lot longer than a day. You heard what Jed said."

His mother told Blue, "You're welcome to stay here as long as you need to. But we do have to get in touch with somebody to let them know you're safe. The county sheriff might be able to reach your uncle even if he is traveling."

Tibo murmured, "I sure wouldn't mind stayin'."

Blue told the Colters, "It's awfully nice here but we have to take off—in the morning. I'll just have to leave the *Victory* here and then my uncle and I can come back and get it when it's fixed. He'll pay for everything. Tibo and I can hitchhike to the city tomorrow." That plan had come to her in a flash; it seemed an almost perfect answer.

"Hitchhike!" Mrs. Colter exclaimed. "You'll do no such thing. It's too dangerous. Let *me* try to call your uncle. Just give me his number, dear." She pushed back her chair with an air of determination.

Blue fidgeted with her napkin. Stalling, she made a show of investigating her pockets. "I had it on a scrap of paper—I must have left it by the 'phone. I'll go look."

Jed had just finished his call. "All yours," he said as Blue reached the office. He went whistling toward the dining room.

Blue groaned. She had really trapped herself this time with her lies. She reached for a memo pad by the telephone, thinking to scribble down any number that came to mind. No, that would only tighten the trap. For a desperate moment she considered telling the whole truth. Only, then the Colters would know what a terrible deceiver she was. She visualized Harley's clear blue eyes staring at her in shock.

His mother came to the doorway. "Can't you find it, Linda?"

Blue pretended to search among bits of scribbled memoranda, then in the waste basket. "Oh, I remember! I think I gave it to Tibo, for some reason. He loses everything."

"But don't you remember the number?"

"I've an awfully poor memory for numbers."

"Well, surely you know your uncle's address. I'll simply call the operator." She regarded Blue with a perplexed gaze.

Blue thought quickly. To say that she couldn't remember Uncle Stewart's address would be going too far. "Its—uh—2534 Garfield. I think."

Mrs. Colter's forefinger went to the dial. "And the phone is listed under the name of Stewart Lincoln?"

"Yes'm," Blue croaked. "I mean, I guess so—unless it's been changed. The last time he wrote he said something about moving somewhere else."

"When did he write last? You say he did know you were coming?"

"Oh, yes. Only—well, it took me longer to get ready than I expected. So, I guess it's a few weeks since the letter. And—well, there are acts of God, and all."

Mrs. Colter gave her another long look, then dialed. She asked the operator, "Could you please tell me if there is a Stewart Lincoln listed at 2534 Garfield, Minneapolis?"

Blue closed her eyes. Everything was going wrong. She had planned to look in the Minneapolis directory herself when she got there and find his address for certain, or consult one of the Travelers' Aid people she had heard about. Then she would go right to her uncle's. He'd see how much she resembled her dead father! He would know and welcome her at once. But now. . . .

"Thank you, operator," Mrs. Colter said. She hung up, wrote on the memo pad, then passed it to Blue. "There you are."

Blue stared at the paper. Five hundred ten Edgemont. Below it was a telephone number.

"So you were right, Linda. He has moved." She gave Blue's shoulder an encouraging pat. "I'll leave you to talk to him privately. Give him our name and address here: R.D. One, Lake Center, and be sure to tell him that if he wants to arrange for bus tickets, if he can't drive down, Maurice and I will take care of that. Do you need any help dialing?"

"No, ma'am. Thank you," Blue managed.

Alone, she stared at the memo slip again.

Edgemont. It had an elegant sound. There was a payphone booth in Chicksaw and for a dime she could have called the operator and gotten this information herself. She was as ignorant as Tibo.

She touched the dial then drew back. Calling was a lot different from going up to Uncle Stewart's house in person. She could pretend to the Colters that the line was busy or that no one answered. But they would urge her to keep on trying. Taking a deep breath, she spun the dial with a trembling forefinger.

There were three rings at the other end.

"Yes?" a woman's creaky voice responded. In the background was the muffled sound of a radio or television set.

Blueberry's voice seemed lost somewhere in the weak region of her knees. "Uh—I'd like to speak to Mr. Stewart Lincoln, please."

"Who?"

"Mr. Stewart Lincoln. You see, he's my—"

The other voice cut in. It sounded old, reedy, and impatient. "Who's callin'?"

"Linda," Blue quavered. "Though mostly they call me Blueberry."

"Blue—*what?*" the voice demanded. "You look here, whoever you are, I'm sick of being pestered by kids playin' games. Next time, I'm going to get the telephone company after all of you!" There was a click. The line went dead.

Blue replaced the receiver softly. Her cheeks burned as if she had been slapped. Had it been Uncle

Stewart's wife? It couldn't be, not with such an old and stringy voice! It must have been a maid, an aging servant he kept on out of kindness.

She waited until her heart stopped pounding, then braced herself and walked slowly back to the dining room.

"With a customer like Cook," Jed was telling the others, "my boatworks will really hum!"

Blue slipped quietly into her chair, wishing she could go unnoticed forever. The conversation ceased as Mrs. Colter turned to her. "Did you reach him?"

"Somebody else answered—a maid, probably, or a housekeeper—and said he wasn't home."

"But didn't you explain who you were? Your uncle would surely have left a message for you."

"I tried to explain but she couldn't seem to hear very well. There was a TV on. I guess I'd better not try again now, in case he comes home late."

"I'm sure you're disappointed, dear, but Jed has some good news. He was planning to drive to Minneapolis next week but this new customer—he owns half the lake around here—needs a part for his cruiser by tomorrow night."

Jed told Blue, "I'll be leaving in the morning. You and Tibo can ride along."

"That way," Mrs. Colter said, "Jed can see you right to your uncle's door."

"Oh," Blue said, beset by sudden qualms. "But what about the *Victory*, and Hunch?"

Jed leaned back with the confident air of a big business man. "We'll repair the boat and then let you know when it's ready. I'll pick up a new rudder for her tomorrow."

Mr. Colter poured cream into his coffee. "You can leave Hunch with us, Linda, until everything's straightened around. He'll help take the place of the canary here that Marcia used to have." He looked toward his wife. "Billy's cage and stand are still downstairs, aren't they?"

"Of course. I wouldn't throw them away for anything."

Harley stood up. "Before Mom breaks down in tears over Billy, again, let's take a look at your city map, Jed, and locate Mr. Lincoln's address."

As Mrs. Colter removed dishes, Jed spread the map out on the table. Harley and Mr. Colter peered over his shoulder. Blue and Tibo tried to do the same.

"There it is." Harley pointed. "Edgemont. Right off Lyndale."

Jed said, "We were out that way once, Harl, remember?" He shook his head. "But it's a long stretch from where I have to go." He indicated a street far across the city.

Blueberry felt dazed as she looked at the bewildering design of streets, lakes, and boulevards. Would she ever find her way through such a maze? The rude response to her call had shaken her self-confidence. If she didn't watch out she would become as lily-livered as Tibo.

"I seen your pickup truck," Tibo was telling Jed.

"It's sure a neat one. Are we all gonna ride in that?"

"Too crowded," Jed said. "I figured on taking the station wagon." He looking questioningly at his father. "Okay, Dad?"

Mr. Colter ran a finger back and forth under his nose, thinking. "Well, anything for the Jed Colter Boatworks."

Harley said to Blue, "Man, I wish I could ride along tomorrow. Only, I need the money from the job. I want to buy myself a sailboat before the summer's over."

"Tad always wanted a sailboat," Blue said.

"Who's Tad?" Mrs. Colter asked.

"My big brother."

"I thought you said all your relatives were dead, except your uncle."

Blue had difficulty remembering just what she *had* said. To be a good liar one had to have a very good memory. "Oh—well, yes. But I didn't mean Tad; just our parents. Tad's grown up. He went to Alaska. Before he left we built the boat and we were going to sail it down the Mississippi some day."

Mr. Colter started carrying his plate into the kitchen. "Workers made a lot of money up there when the oil pipeline was being built. Probably still some good jobs to be had."

"Well, Linda," Mrs. Colter said, "I'm relieved to learn you're not all alone in the world. Having a brother, I mean."

I might as well be alone, Blue thought, and sought

to escape from a wave of sadness over Tad by making herself useful. "I'll help you do the dishes, Mrs. Colter." Jed and Harley disappeared into the kitchen with their own stack of plates.

"I've a better idea," Mrs. Colter said. She called to Harley. "Harley, go show Linda and Tibo around the resort."

Tibo hesitated. "Jed said he was gonna go someplace in his pickup and that I could ride with him."

"I know where that someplace is," Harley said, coming back from the kitchen. "His girl friend's. Good idea for him to have a chaperone. How about you, Linda—want to have a look around?"

She nodded, not certain what she wanted to do.

When Harley went upstairs to get a sweater, she had a chance to take Tibo aside. "You keep mum, Tibo, if Jed or anybody asks questions. Don't tell any more than you have to."

Tibo nodded, then shrugged. "It's great here. But I sure wonder what's gonna happen later."

Harley returned and he and Blue walked slowly around the resort. Harley pointed out a sundial he had constructed in the center of a lawn bordered by flower beds and varnished log cabins.

"Hey, look at the sunset," he said, pausing near the dock. "It's as orange as the oriole Mom tamed last year, back in Wisconsin where we used to live. D'you want to take a ride in the canoe before it gets dark?"

"That would be nice," Blue said.

She waited on the dock while Harley brought the

silvery canoe near. The lake, the sunset, a thrush singing, one early star faintly visible; all of it was so lovely she wanted the moment never to end. Just in case something went wrong in Minneapolis, perhaps she could come back here and stay. She could be a big help doing chores, and maybe even learn to sail with Harley when he bought his sailboat.

He was drifting alongside the dock now, his tan skin and blond hair accentuated by a dark blue sweater. He held one hand up to her to help her down into the canoe.

In the canoe, Blueberry leaned back on a cushioned backrest, facing Harley. She felt like a queen.

"It's beautiful here," she said shyly. "And your folks, and Jed, are really nice."

"They're not bad," Harley admitted. "Except for Jed's being so girl crazy."

"Do you have a girl friend?"

"Well—not really. It's hard to get acquainted in a new place. We only moved here this spring. Anyhow, I'm not going to go messing up my life with a bunch of romance and stuff. I'm too busy with important things."

"That's the way I feel too!" She was amazed at how much they seemed to have in common in spite of his being older and their differences in background.

"There is this one girl I date sometimes," he confessed, then shrugged. "Not that it's important."

She felt let down, almost betrayed, and was silent.

From the edge of the lake came the wild-woman-laugh of a loon. Both she and Harley looked to see a black, winged bird soar in silhouette against the fading sunlight.

"A loon call always gives me goose pimples," Blue said.

"Me too." Harley feathered the oar. She studied how he did it, envying his skill. "I guess we'd better start circling back. We'll have to be up early in the morning."

"I don't need much sleep," she said, but he was already paddling homeward.

Nearing shore, Harley said, "Maybe I could come and see you and Tibo once in a while in the city, whenever I ride in with Jed. We have a cousin there."

"Or we could write to each other. I don't have anybody to write to—except Uncle Stewart. In the past, I mean."

"I'm not very good at writing. I get the worst grades in that."

"I'm not too good at it myself. But my brother wrote wonderful things; stories and even poems."

"Yeah? Well—I hope everything turns out fine for you at your uncle's. If it doesn't—you heard Mom say you'd be welcome here."

She trailed a finger in the water. "Yes, but I couldn't stay forever."

"No, I suppose not."

He beached the canoe and they walked toward the large main building that served as the Colters' living quarters, resort recreation center, and general lodge.

The music of a harmonica drifted across the evening air.

Blue felt a flash of anger. Tibo must have sneaked her harmonica into his pocket. She would give him a piece of her mind! The music sounded nice, though. Her anger softened. Little Tibo hadn't had many chances in life to enjoy himself.

"Jed's back early," Harley commented. "He always does a stint with his harmonica when he's feeling good."

Jed! Blue apologized mentally to Tibo.

Harley held the lodge's entrance door open for her and then led the way into a large room equipped with tables for billiards, Ping-Pong, and bridge. On a sofa sat Jed and Tibo. Jed cradled a harmonica against his mouth. Tibo sat in fascinated silence, listening to what he played.

A familiar squawk made Blue wheel. There was Hunch, his cage hanging from an ornamental brass standard. The tone of his squawk hinted that he was warming up to shout something outrageous. She felt her nerves tighten.

Jed lowered the harmonica and spoke to Tibo. "This is a chromatic. When you want to shift to a minor key you push in this slide knob. D'you want to give it a try?"

"Gee! Could I? Yeah!" Tibo took the harmonica and blew into it experimentally.

Harley said, "Seems we're interrupting a concert."

Jed and Tibo looked up. Hunch turned too. One

bead-round eye fixed on Blueberry. She held her breath.

"I'll be damned!" he rasped. "Awr-kk! Pass the spuds. Dammit. Awr-kk! Did somebody let a . . . ?"

Her face burning, Blue ran toward the cage. "Shut up, you old fool bird!" She gave the cage a shake to try to stop Hunch before he blatted out things that would betray her even more. As it was she imagined that Jed and Harley could see through all her pretenses, even to visualizing the tar paper shack and Pa spitting tobacco juice. She forced herself to face them and stammered, "I'm sorry—the kids at the orphanage taught him a lot of bad things."

Harley seemed not to hear, covering a grin with his hand. Jed laughed out loud.

Tibo bragged, "He can say even worse things!"

Blue wished the floor would open up and swallow him and her both. She dimly heard Harley urge the parrot, "Okay, Hunch, how about giving us the works?"

Jed added, "Right on! Linda, you ought to put that bird on TV—but not on a kids' program, I guess. Come on, Hunch. Tibo said you could do worse."

Blue marveled. Maybe Tibo had said the right thing accidentally, fatal though it had seemed. Best, Hunch was suddenly silent. "He's as contrary as a mule," she told Harley and Jed. "I try to teach him nice words but. . . ." Her voice trailed off. She felt desperately tired, eager only for escape. "I'll cover his cage now so he goes to sleep." She did, hastily, then ordered Tibo, "We're going to our own cabin now."

"It's early," Harley protested. "How about some hot chocolate?"

"Thanks—but it's been a long day." Dragging a protesting Tibo, she left. Outside, she said, "You about blew everything."

He looked at her, his eyes shining innocently in the first starlight. "The only thing I blew was Jed's harmonica." He sighed, glancing back at the lodge. "We really had fun today, didn't we, Blue?"

She forced herself to silence. Well, there had been once nice thing for her: the canoe ride with Harley.

Day of Discovery

WIND FROM THE CAR'S SIDE WINDOW fanned Blueberry's hair. From time to time, she brushed a lock from her eyes while she stared out at an unreal world. The world was real enough, she knew: the lakes, rivers, small towns, the farms with their silos and barns. The sense of unreality was in *her*. At one place where Jed sent the station wagon across a long bridge spanning the Mississippi, she gazed down at the brown water and seemed to see the *Victory*, or its ghost, still sailing onward.

"Is that Minneapolis?" Tibo called from the back

seat as a cluster of buildings appeared on the horizon.

"Not yet," Jed said. "Pretty soon, though. You'll be able to tell by all the tall buildings. There's a real skyscraper there now, the IDS building. It makes the old Foshay tower a midget."

"I saw a picture of it once," Blue boasted.

"I like tall pines better than tall buildings," Jed said. "Not that a city isn't exciting. You'll probably like living there, a lot, once you get used to it."

Tibo said, "I'm gonna look in all the big store windows and pretend I kin buy anything I want!" He kept leaning across the seat so far that Blue could feel his breath on her cheek.

"If you aren't careful," she warned, "you'll end up in my lap!"

"You're supposed to have your seat belt on," Jed said.

Tibo made a mocking sound. "I ain't scared."

A short while later the city's skyline came into view: towers, stacks, roofs, bridges, and an increasing maze of highways.

"Wow!" Tibo exclaimed frequently, along with, "Hey, look! What's that? Where're we now?"

Blueberry was mostly silent, feeling both awe and apprehension. The traffic around them increased so that it seemed the station wagon was part of a roaring, mechanical stream.

Blue glanced at Jed's profile, searching for the right words. "I know you're in a big hurry, Jed, and you said my uncle's place is a long way from where you have to go. You can just leave me and Tibo off somewhere and we'll find our way."

"Mom expects me to see you to the door."

"But you don't have to." She didn't want Jed to see her meeting with her uncle. What if nothing turned out at all as she had planned? All her lies could come home to roost—awful, crowing, feathered things cawing the truth. A crowd of black crows chanting, "Haw—haw!"

"I heard you and Harley talk about a bus that runs close to Uncle Stewart's address," she persisted. "Why can't Tibo and I just get on that?"

Jed glanced at his wristwatch. "I am running late," he admitted. "Saturday traffic seems even worse than usual. But, still. . . . Mom would blow her top if you got lost or anything happened."

"We wouldn't get lost! If we got turned around or something we could always ask somebody, like a policeman."

"I won't ask the cops nothin'," Tibo mumbled.

Jed ran a finger back and forth under his nose, like his father. "Well, there is a bus—stops a block from your uncle's place. Safe enough, I guess, but. . . ."

"If I'm going to live in the city I have to start learning, don't I? It would be exciting; I've never been on a big bus." She paused. "Anyhow, I think my uncle would like to see me by himself when we first meet. You know."

Jed was silent, debating his decision. Then,

abruptly, he said, "Okay. We're on a main avenue now. Hennepin. You can catch a bus here and it'll take you right along Lyndale to Edgemont. First, I have to find a parking lot. Then I'll draw a map and give you a 'phone number where you can reach me so I can let the folks know you're okay. Or maybe I should check back in person, so's I can give Mom a firsthand account."

"There's nothing to worry about," Blue protested. "It would be silly for you to take extra time to drive to Edgemont." She pushed away the nagging memory of the sour voice on the telephone. "Everything's going to be A-okay!"

Jed found a parking lot, turned in, and stopped the car. There he drew a crude map, with written instructions, and added the 'phone number where he could be reached, saying, "Give me a ring, Linda. Any time before about three o'clock." He smiled his nice smile. "Otherwise, I'll drop by."

"It's out of your way," she said. "I'll call you."

He tapped the map. "Does it seem clear?"

"I'd have to be a real bumpkin to get lost, with that."

"You and Tibo follow me."

They had barely reached the bus stop when Jed said, "There's the bus you want, heading this way. Hurry."

Dodging through the other pedestrians, the three made their way to the curb. Jed dug into his pocket, then dumped a number of coins into Blue's hand. He studied her. "You're sure? I mean, if you're nervous. . . ."

"About what?" Blue countered. She pulled Tibo into the line of waiting passengers. She watched the bus door swing wide.

"Move it!" somebody behind her urged, prodding her and Tibo up the bus steps.

"Drop the money in the fare box," the driver said.

From a dry throat, she squeezed out, "How much?"

He jabbed a finger toward a sign that clearly stated the fare.

Blue fumbled, her face scorched, bodies pressing against her. A coin spun to the floor and out of sight. Blue dived after it.

"I don't have all day," the driver said. "Look for it later."

She counted out the remaining coins, then dropped the proper amount into the fare box.

"D'you want a transfer?"

She looked at the driver blankly. "I don't know, sir."

"Well, where are you going? The address!" She faltered out the information. "You don't need a transfer. Go back and sit down. I'll tell you when we get to Edgemont."

"Th-thank you," she stammered and crouched to try to find the lost coin. Oncoming passengers pushed her off balance. She gave up the search, then fled with Tibo to a vacant seat at the rear of the bus.

Tibo bounced up and down on the springy seat. "Hey, this is neat."

A young woman tapped Blue's shoulder. "Here—your dime rolled right under my feet."

Blue took the dime, too stunned to say thanks. Pa always claimed that the city was full of people who cheated or stole, or knocked you over the head for money. Some did, of course. He said most of the world was that way. Maybe. But there were people like the Colters and Lena Finch, too. And it wasn't as if everybody in Chicksaw Landing was a saint! Just the opposite. Mostly, they were too scared and shiftless to go to the big cities and try to make something of themselves.

A sense of pride filled her as the bus moved on. She was different! A Lincoln, she reminded herself, as excitement and anticipation replaced her earlier anxiety.

She busied herself studying how other passengers pulled a signal cord when they wanted to get off, and how they pushed open a side, exit door.

Tibo, on the inside seat, was fiddling with a window latch. He slid the window open and grinned at her. "I made it work right off!"

"You want to blast us out of here?" a man roared behind them. "Shut that damn thing!"

Tibo struggled with the window. It refused to

budge. The man leaned forward, muttering, and pushed it shut.

"Don't go monkeying with things," Blue admonished Tibo. "You sit quietly and behave now. Especially when we reach Uncle Stew's. Jed said it was about fifteen blocks."

She tried to count the blocks, studying the scenes the bus passed. There was a large cathedral, then a green park with a rippling pond where ducks and a swan swam. There were tennis courts and a place where people played croquet.

"We're getting to where the rich people live," she confided to Tibo.

The bus climbed a hill and swerved off Hennepin onto Lyndale. Instead of a park or cathedrals, there were clusters of business places, drive-ins, garages, and even beer parlors. Most of the structures looked dingy and old, with apartment houses here and there. Soon, Blue was sure, there would be nice houses and lawns once the bus was through this section.

The bus slowed. "Edgemont," the driver called.

Blueberry sat unmoving, certain she had not heard right. There was a drugstore on one corner, a hamburger place on the other, a gasoline station, a coin laundry.

"Edgemont, you kids!" the driver repeated, jerking around in his seat.

Blue and Tibo stumbled out to the corner. The bus

grumbled onward, leaving a blue gust of exhaust behind it.

"It looks kinda crummy around here," Tibo said.

"We have to walk a ways," Blue told him but there was a hollowness at the pit of her stomach. She took Jed's map from her blouse pocket. Straight ahead, up a slight hill, was Edgemont. Only one block to 510, Jed had said.

"Come on," she told Tibo.

A car horn blared, brakes squealed, and a passing driver shouted, "Wait for the signal, dummy!"

Blue retreated to the curb, yanking Tibo with her, only now observing the red signal light. "As if I didn't know we had to wait 'til it turned green!" she snorted to hide her embarrassment. "I didn't notice, that's all. Even people who live here can get absentminded."

"People keep yellin' at us," Tibo grumbled, "just like at the Home."

"Well—they're busy and in a big hurry. That's the way we'll be when we're city people."

The light turned green and they started on their way up the incline. "It's probably a long block before we reach Uncle Stewart's where things get nice again. Now, you let me do all the talking. You nearly spilled the beans back at the Colters."

"How did I know you were going to tell all them lies?" There was black accusation in his glance. "You said people shouldn't lie."

"They shouldn't, usually, but sometimes. . . . Oh, I don't want to talk about it. I have to keep my mind on more important matters." She studied a house number. Five hundred. Uncle Stewart's house could not be much farther on. Only, there was no handsome mansion in sight, nor a park with swans, not even a yard full of grass.

"It must be about lunch time," Tibo said. "Maybe your uncle will give us a good meal, huh?"

She scarcely heard. There, to her left, the number "510" showed clearly on the eave of a weathered porch. The large house was a grim gray-white, with faded shingles topping its three stories. One of the porch pillars leaned. There was a small patch of grass above a retaining wall but it was as scrawny and defeated-looking as the grass back home. Glass wind chimes hanging from the porch ceiling made a thin, tinkling sound in the faint breeze.

"What're we stoppin' here for, Blue?"

Blueberry consulted the map again. "Maybe Mrs. Colter made a mistake when she wrote the address down. Probably it was six hundred ten." She started onward, Tibo following.

At the end of the six hundred block, with only more dreary buildings ahead, Blue stopped.

"I guess that was his place, back there," she admitted. "It's probably real nice inside."

She led the way up the outside steps to the porch and to two doors beyond. On the wall beside the doors were several mailboxes. On one was a name: Alma Lincoln. Underneath was a doorbell.

Blue licked her dry lips, then pressed the bell. Her heart pounded.

Tibo said in an undertone. "Maybe there ain't nobody home. Maybe your uncle hasn't got back yet."

"Sh-h-h!" There was a creaking of floorboards. The doorknob rattled, turned. The door opened only a few inches. "What do you want?" a voice demanded.

"I—" Blue's voice stuck in her throat. She could make out, dimly, a long-jawed face, gray hair pulled back into a bun, eyes peering suspiciously through thick-lensed spectacles. "I—I'm looking for Stewart Lincoln. I called on the 'phone last night. My name's Linda—Blueberry." Her hand strayed to the necklace. "Uncle Stewart sent me this."

The eyes behind the glasses measured her. "So you're the one who called, eh? Why didn't you say so then?" Her gaze went to Tibo. "What's that boy doin' with you?"

"He's—uh—a friend. You see, we thought . . ."

The woman continued to study her through the narrow opening. Then there was the sound of a chain lock being unfastened. The door opened wider. "So you're Stewart's niece Linda, is that it? I can see the resemblance in the eyes and chin. Well, what're you doin' here?"

Blueberry swallowed, studying the woman more fully now. She was tall. A loose cotton dress hung from her stooped shoulders. She had on felt carpet slippers. A cat meowed from the unseen recesses of a room behind her and although the cat voice was nothing like Smith's, Blue felt a pang.

She recovered her own voice. "I—we—dropped by to say hello. I was hoping Uncle Stewart would be here."

The woman looked at her strangely and then led the way through a small lobby, past a telephone stand, a potted fern, and an ancient, velvet-covered chair, toward a doorway.

"You can go in here."

Tibo hung back, glancing nervously about, then followed Blue's hesitant lead into a large living room where drawn curtains kept out the sunlight.

"Set down," the woman ordered, indicating a faded settee where a cat lay. "Get up, Homer." The elegant cat had buff-colored fur and pale blue eyes.

"I had a cat once," Blue said, looking toward the woman in the hope that liking cats could establish some warmth between them. "I love cats!"

The woman only grunted. It seemed she had not heard. Perhaps she was somewhat deaf, Blue reasoned, speaking loudly. "He doesn't have to move. I'll. . . ." She went to a cracked leather chair nearby. "This is fine."

Tibo looked around, at a loss, then moved to Blue as if for protection.

"There's a footstool right under your nose, boy," the woman pointed out.

"Oh, yeah—thank you, ma'am." Tibo crouched on the stool, shrinking into himself.

The woman sat down beside the cat, her eyes on Blueberry. "So you're Thaddeus's girl. I recollect them beads you're wearing. I helped Stewart pick them out. And some perfume too. Where's your brother? Stewart used to mention him. Older, wasn't he?"

Blue nodded. "Tad," she said.

The woman gazed into space as if she saw something there no one else could see. "Stewart and Thaddeus were very close. It shook him up when Thaddeus died. Stewart kept saying he should send something to Thaddeus's little girl. But he never knew if you got the package he did send. He thought you'd at least write and thank him."

"I did write," Blue said and explained about the difficulty with the address. Outside, there was the rumble of traffic shuttling past.

"Yes, him and Thaddeus were very close," the aging woman mused.

Homer jumped down and stared up at Blue out of blue, steady eyes.

Blueberry cleared her throat. "Are you—Alma Lincoln?"

"That's my name on the mailbox, ain't it?"

Tibo, on the sly, tweaked the cat's tail.

Alma Lincoln's glasses glinted in his direction. "You leave Homer be!" She swiveled her head toward Blue. "Where's your brother now, then?"

"He went away for a while. He got a good job out west. He's doing real well, he writes."

"Lucky, then. So many young people are out of work. Are your folks living here in the city now? Stewart and me thought maybe all of you were dead or had left the country, never hearing from anybody."

"Ma doesn't write to anybody hardly. And not knowing for certain what your address was. Fairfield or Garfield."

"Garfield," Alma Lincoln said. "We moved from there almost two years ago. Now, what did you say about wanting to see your uncle—what did you mean, if that was it? I don't always hear too good."

"Well, I—I thought. . . ." Her voice quavered. "I need to see him to tell him about—well, everything. Where is he?" She waited, twisting her feet, appeal in her eyes.

Alma Lincoln made a sound, not a laugh, not a cry, but something in between. "He's out in the Lakewood graveyard. Has been for almost a year now."

Blue sat transfixed. She studied the red and yellow embroidery on a table runner as if it were the most important thing in the world. She heard herself say, "His name was in the 'phone book."

As from a great distance Alma Lincoln's voice replied, "I just ain't bothered to put it under my own name yet. If I ever do. Safer to have it under a man's name on account of obscene calls."

"Hey, look at the cat!" Tibo exclaimed. "He's gettin' ready to jump up in my lap. I guess he likes me."

Blue looked only at Alma Lincoln. "You mean—Uncle Stewart's dead?"

"He wouldn't be in the graveyard if he wasn't."

The cat moved from Tibo to Blue. Mechanically, her eyes and throat hot with unshed tears, she bent and stroked the animal, not really seeing it or anything else. Uncle Stewart dead!

Tibo sat blinking, seeming finally to have comprehended what had been said.

"There wasn't any way I could be sure of reaching you," the woman continued, "not knowing for sure where you were. Homer, you go lay down and stop pestering."

"He's not bothering me," Blue said if only for something to say. It did not matter much anymore what she said or even thought. Uncle Stewart was dead. The *Victory* was wrecked. The whole dream was smashed. Even the necklace she wore was a kind of glass lie.

"How did you come to the city—I mean, are your folks with you? Your ma married again, I heard years back."

"My folks are back home, up north in Chicksaw Landing. Tibo and I got a ride with a friend. We—uh. . . ." She looked around, vacant-eyed. What to do or say next? It was impossible to think in this airless, suddenly suffocating room. She stood up abruptly. "We—have to be going. Uh—it was nice to meet you. I didn't know Uncle Stewart was married."

"My land, child! I'm Stewart's sister. Your aunt.

Him and his wife broke up when they were still back in Springfield, long ago."

"Oh," Blue said. She heard herself babbling mindlessly, "Tad and I were always hoping we could go to Springfield someday. I've never been to Illinois or any other place outside of Minnesota. We were going to look up the records there and find out just how we were related to Abraham Lincoln."

"Illinois! I'm talkin' about Springfield, Minnesota, a little town in the southwestern part of the state. Us Lincolns ain't related to any president. Stewart's and my grandfather—your dad's too—came over from England. Where did you ever hear such nonsense?"

It didn't seem there was enough of her dream left to break but she imagined she heard a final, splintering sound above the slur of traffic.

"Uh—could I use your 'phone, please?" Jed had mentioned coming by to see how things were if she didn't call him. Even though she would have to tell him the truth on the phone—or some part of it—she couldn't bear for him to see this house or Aunt Alma. Above all, she could not stay here. She would have to go back to the Colters and then. . . ?

Her aunt waved a hand. "The 'phone's in the hall there. But I think I heard Mr. Bestland—he's one of my roomers—come down to use it."

Tibo sat fidgeting uneasily on the hassock. His stomach rumbled loudly enough to be heard. Blue looked toward him, feeling remorse on top of her guilt.

Tibo sniffed. "Somethin' sure smells good."

An old-fashioned wall clock gonged twelve times. Alma checked the clock's time against that of a small, gold timepiece pinned to the front of her dress. "That big clock hasn't lost or gained a minute in forty years." She stood. "I always eat right at twelve noon. I reckon there's enough soup to share, if you've got the time."

Tibo told Blue, "Jed said he wouldn't be ready until about three."

"You must've heard wrong," Blue countered. To her aunt she said, "Thank you but we both had big breakfasts. As soon as I make my call we have to leave."

"Gee, Blue," Tibo protested, "I can eat soup in a real hurry."

"Suit yourselves," Alma Lincoln said. "But if you have to wait for Mr. Bestland to finish talking you'll have time for three meals." She went toward the kitchen.

Tibo gave Blue a brief, defiant glance, and followed.

Alone in the room, Blue studied a display of framed photographs on a table near the front window. One was of a man in a military uniform. The man had a square chin, laugh lines down his cheeks, and dreamy eyes. Across the bottom of the picture was written, "Greetings from Italy. Love, Stew." He looked like her father, she thought. And a little like Tad too. The other photographs were of persons she did not know.

Oh, Uncle Stew, she grieved silently. I would have liked you, I know. Maybe you would have learned to like me too.

She heard the stairs creak and went out to see the roomer hobbling up the stairs to his quarters. Removing Jed's instructions from her pocket she went to the telephone. She lifted the receiver, then hesitated. She hadn't really thought through anything clearly. Jed might not even be at the boat supply shop yet, it being way over on the other side of town. Or, if he were, he might be alarmed and rush right over if she called so soon. She replaced the receiver.

The large front room seemed even dimmer and lonelier when she slipped back in. Homer had followed his mistress to the kitchen. Smith would not be happy here, Blue thought. He could never be a city cat penned up in a stuffy apartment.

Aunt Alma suddenly appeared, a stark shadow against the light of a rear window. ""There's still some soup left, if you've changed your mind."

Blueberry considered. She wasn't truly hungry but it was hard to tell when she and Tibo would have a chance to eat again. Not soon, anyhow. "I guess I could eat a little."

The kitchen, to her surprise, was pleasant. Sunny with flower-splashed curtains, and a small wall clock that sounded less doleful than the one in the front room. The woman filled a soup bowl and brought it to her, together with some dark bread.

"Young Tibo here is quite a talker," Aunt Alma said, seating herself back at her own place. "So you planned to come here and live with your uncle."

Blue shot Tibo a look of near hatred. She managed a shrug. "It was only pretending. Why, Ma would be heartbroken if I left home. Pa, too."

"Is he a good man?"

"He's real nice."

"How about your ma? Is she still as flighty as she used to be? She certainly led your father on a merry chase."

"Oh, she's just fine," Blue answered between sips of thin soup.

"Is your soup all right?" her aunt asked.

"Very good," Blue responded, sensing a note of appeal in the woman's reedy voice.

"Stewart always said I could make wonderful soup out of almost nothing." She stroked the oilcloth on the table. "I don't know what you had in mind, coming here. I couldn't afford an extra mouth."

Blue tried to look astonished. "Goodness, Aunt Alma, I didn't really expect anything. Tibo tells a lot of tall tales. He's only six."

"I'm almost nine!" Tibo declared.

"Whatever you say," Blue responded, resigned. "I arranged for Jed to pick us up downtown." She would tell him the truth when they were by themselves. "We'll have time to look in the store windows and things beforehand." She asked her aunt, "Do we take the same bus back downtown?"

"Yes. They run quite often." She got up from the table, brushing at the front of her dress. "Now I have to feed Homer. Then we both take a nice nap. Look at him sittin' there on the windowsill drooling over a sparrow outside." She smiled fondly.

At the door where the woman let them out, Blue said, "Well, good-bye. Thanks for the good soup."

Alma reached into her apron pocket. "One of my tenants gave me some chocolates at Easter. There's a few left over. Here." She handed one to Blue, one to Tibo.

The two started down the steps to the sidewalk below.

Aunt Alma called after Blue, "If you'd like to write to me sometimes, it's nice to get mail."

"I will," Blue promised.

She and Tibo walked slowly on. He took small nibbles of his chocolate, treasuring each bite.

"What're we going to do now, Blue?" he asked. "With your uncle dead. I guess you didn't know what you were talking about, did you?"

"And I don't want to talk about it now. I have to think. Hard. Remember that park we went by? Close enough to walk to."

"But you said we were going downtown to look at things. And that Jed was gonna pick us up there."

"I didn't call him," she confessed. "Tibo—I don't know what to do now!" To her shame, a tear ran down one cheek.

He looked at her. "There ain't nothing to do but go back and stay with the Colters, is there? And fix up the *Victory* like we planned. Then. . . ." His voice trailed off, his expression questioning.

She brushed at her eyes. "Don't rush me. I'll think it all through. In the park." She saw the dark disappointment in his eyes. "All right. Downtown. I've got an idea hatching."

"Your ideas sure flopped before. You said your uncle was expectin' you—and me too." He kicked at a bottle cap lying on the sidewalk.

"Haven't you ever made a mistake?"

Silent, he trudged on beside her, hands in his pockets. "I guess I won't ever get to be a captain or anything."

"There you go self-pitying yourself again." Less harshly, she added, "We'll make out somehow. A person has to keep hanging onto a dream, or find a new one, when the first one smashes. This isn't the end of everything."

"Seems pretty close to it."

She saw their bus approaching and seized his hand. "Come on, Tibo. I'll call Jed from downtown. And when he picks us up at the parking lot I'll try to explain to him about what happened. Damn right we'll fix up the *Victory!* My new idea's pecking its way out of the shell already. We'll head back upriver."

"Back to Chicksaw?"

"No," she said firmly and waved at the oncoming bus as if she were flagging down a train.

Flight by Moonlight

BLUEBERRY SAT ON THE LONG SOFA IN the Colter recreation room, Tibo beside her. Faces—Harley's, his parents'—were turned toward her.

Her cheeks burning, she struggled on through a confession of the truth, or some of it. "I—I didn't want to rot away in Brush Falls for the rest of my life. And then when Tad left. . . ."

At the mention of Brush Falls, Mrs. and Mr. Colter exchanged a look.

Blue blundered on. "Our boat that we'd built, the

Victory, was like, well, it seemed it could be like a magical chariot. Something that would take me to, you know, some place wonderful." She appealed. "I didn't know Uncle Stewart was dead."

"I'm sure you didn't, Linda," Mrs. Colter said. "But I'm afraid you made up a few things."

Blue's hands twisted in her lap. "All the kids—at the orphanage—dream up things, even crazier than I did. About having rich or famous relatives somewhere. They lie about it all the time. I must've caught the habit, even though I know it's a terrible one."

Harley's father said, "Jed already told us a few things before he went out on his date tonight, about your conversation in the car on the way back. He didn't think he was betraying a confidence."

There was an "I told you so" look in Tibo's eyes, his expression plainly revealing that his motto of never trusting anybody was the only sensible one to follow.

"I told Jed," Blue said, "that I was going to tell you the truth about everything."

"And have you?" Mr. Colter asked.

She felt doubly uncomfortable under his searching gaze. "Maybe I've left out a few little things."

Mrs. Colter's voice was warm but her eyes were as probing as her husband's. "I do know what it's like to want to run away. I tried it once when I was about your age but I went scurrying home the moment it started to grow dark. And I also know that children create pleasant fantasies, even to imagining that a fairy godmother will rescue them from things that are unpleasant. Apparently you believed, or wanted to believe, a little harder than most." She paused and looked uncertainly toward her husband.

"I guess that was it," Blueberry said, wishing that they would let her go.

But Mrs. Colter was looking at her again, intently. "I should explain—you see, Blueberry, Maurice and I guessed that you and Tibo were runaways, although we couldn't tell whether the story about your uncle was actual or a fantasy you had convinced yourself was true."

Blueberry! They had always called her Linda before. She glanced toward Harley. He sat on a hassock pretending to be totally absorbed in tying a shoelace.

"So we," Mrs. Colter went on, "we had to—oh, you tell her the rest, Maurice."

Mr. Colter ran his finger briskly back and forth under his nose. "To make a long story short, Blueberry—Linda—I tried to call the orphanage you mentioned in Brush Falls. I learned that the only orphanage in the county is at Chicksaw Landing."

He paused, waiting for her to say something. She sat stiff, silent, staring at the floor.

"If I had talked to the old timers around here," he went on, "I would have known about the Chicksaw institution. This area is still new to me, you see. Well, I called the Home, as it seems to be called. The director there, a Mr. Bert, said he would go and tell your folks. Which he did. He called me back later. Everyone was worried; at least your mother certainly was. I believe that some radio bulletins were made and arrangements for a formal searching party."

Blue continued to stare at the floor, trying to concentrate on the inlaid cork tile, counting the squares. The only thing she must not do was to cry! That would be the final disgrace.

Mrs. Colter came and put an arm around her. "Now, now, dear, it isn't the end of the world. You're safe, the boys will repair your boat, and then you can sail back upriver with Harley to help you. The man at the orphanage suggested a bus—or we could drive you—but we knew you'd want to return to your home in your own boat."

Tibo sat in fixed silence, his dark eyes moving from one person to another.

Blueberry exclaimed, "I don't need any help sailing the *Victory!* Except for some stuff to repair it with. Tibo and I can fix it and we can sail it together too!"

"We'll talk about it more in the morning," Mrs. Colter said. "You must understand that we had to do what we did, as responsible adults."

"You didn't either have to!" Blue sprang to her feet. "You went behind my back and now—now you've ruined everything!" She ran from the room and across the yard to the privacy of the small cabin she and Tibo shared. There she flung herself onto one of the twin beds and let the tears come.

Nobody followed her. The pale light of dusk faded, blue-purple darkness gradually took over. A loon cried. A distant mourning dove repeated its melancholy song, over and over.

It seemed to her that she hadn't felt so lonely since the time when Tad left. Lonely and defeated. The sad-voiced evening calls of birds were no help. The only thing that would help, at least a little bit, would be Smith's peaceful, singing purr, his warm fur under her hand. Smith was the one she could always talk to, the one to whom she could tell her dreams. And her heartbreak too.

Oh, Smith, honey, she mourned silently, why did you go and leave me like everybody else?

She thought of the pampered Homer with hate.

The hate made her feel a trifle better. And now there were no tears left, not even when she tried to squeeze a few remaining drops from her puffed lids. She found some tissue and blew her nose. An outdoor yard light tossed her image against the mirror of a vanity stand and she stared at her reflection with scorn. The person mirrored there did not look like Blueberry Lincoln Flynn.

She blew her nose again. She would show them all! The Colters, the snotty bus driver, the uppity city people, everybody. "Damn right!" she declared to the mirror and stuck out her tongue.

There was a hesitant knock at the door. Harley's voice asked, "Are you all right, Linda?"

"Why wouldn't I be?"

"Can I come in?"

"What for?" She wiped tear stains from her cheeks.

"I thought maybe—we could talk. I want to say it wasn't my idea to help you sail your boat back. I know you can do it by yourself. I wish you'd let me come in and explain."

"Nobody's stopping you," she said.

Harley entered, stood awkwardly a minute, then sat down on one of the two chairs. "It isn't all Dad's doing. There was a customer in the store this morning. He said somebody from Chicksaw Landing had been by and that there was a searching party being organized for you and Tibo. So, everything would have come out, anyhow."

"So?"

"So, I don't think it's fair to blame my folks for everything."

She met his gaze squarely. "I don't blame anybody except myself. I didn't plan carefully enough, or think things through, that's all. Next time I will! The important thing now is to get the boat fixed up so we can be on our way again. Tibo and me," she added pointedly.

"I know you don't need my help. But you'll never talk my folks into letting you go off alone."

"They don't trust me, isn't that it?"

"Well. Maybe not."

She worked her tongue against the inside of her cheek, thinking, a new scheme rapidly taking shape. "Can we start working on the *Victory* tomorrow?"

"Right. I'll have the whole day free, after church.

Dad's already sorted out some lumber, and there's tons of caulking and stuff in our repair shed." He stood up. "Tibo's practicing on Jed's harmonica, and Mom's going to make some popcorn. Want to come and join everybody?"

"I'll see."

"I wish you would," he said as he left.

She sat for a long while, the plan fattening in her mind until it crowded out almost every other thought. With the details all worked out, she went to the bathroom, dashed cold water on her face, combed her hair carefully, and smoothed out the wrinkles of her blouse. She then closed the door behind her and went toward the lodge, her chin high.

The sun was uncomfortably warm as she and Harley worked on the boat the next morning. In the afternoon, Jed joined them. The *Victory* was pulled free of the water onto a makeshift ways created from two smooth, heavy boards.

"We're coming along faster than I expected," Jed commented. "If we can get some more good licks in tomorrow, after hours, we may have her ready by Tuesday. Wednesday at the latest."

Harley retied the bandana sweat band round his forehead. "I'll arrange with my teachers to take a couple of days off when I go upriver with Linda. Then I'll take a bus back."

Blueberry fitted a piece of fresh planking in place

and said nothing. Tibo stood beside her, handing her tools.

All day Monday, while Harley was in school and Jed at work, she and Tibo continued with some of the smaller repairs. Mrs. Colter had taken them to the site in the speedboat.

"You're really a big help now," Blue told Tibo.

"Honest?"

She looked at him, the sweat under his large eyes, the eager expression. "Honest."

That evening, Harley and Jed once again worked with her, replacing the rudder, putting on the finishing touches, caulking seams, then finally returning the boat to the water where it floated serenely.

"Looks like we can load her up with some supplies tomorrow. Nothing much left now except some minor repairs in the cabin. So, Wednesday morning it is, Linda. How about that?"

"The sooner the better."

Jed challenged, "You don't like it here?"

"That's not it," she said. "It's real nice, nicer than almost any place I've ever seen, but. . . . Well, you know, it's your place, not mine."

"Once you're home," Harley said, "probably that'll seem pretty nice too. I know I'm always glad to get home no matter how good a time I've had away. Like at camp."

She looked at him. He was nice but he was sort of

dumb about real life. She tried to imagine Mr. Colter spitting tobacco juice that sizzled on the stove, and could not.

"I'll make out," was all she said.

The next day, Mrs. Colter took Blue and Tibo to the *Victory* with enough provisions to last a crew of a dozen.

On board the *Victory*, the supplies loaded, she brushed her hands together. "That should keep everybody from going hungry. Harley's appetite is hearty, slim though he is."

"I'm a good eater too," Tibo reminded her.

"I've noticed," Mrs. Colter said with a chuckle. "Linda's the only one who hasn't been cleaning her plate lately."

"I'm too nervous, I guess," Blue said.

"I understand." She touched Blueberry's arm. "You do forgive Maurice and me for doing what we had to do?"

"Yes, ma'am." Blueberry forced herself to add, "I know you meant it for the best."

"It will work out that way, I'm sure. Running away from one's problems is no solution. Now, remember, you'll always be welcome at Pinerest. You and Tibo. You could come spend a whole week or more during summer vacation."

"Thank you. I—we'll—think about it."

Then they were heading back to the resort. As they

approached the line of boats pulled up on shore, Blue studied the silver canoe. The paddle, she knew, was in the boathouse; she had watched Harley place it there. The boathouse door was usually locked but the windows were unlatched and easily opened.

"Harley is so looking forward to this trip with you," Mrs. Colter said above the sound of the launch's engine.

"I know," Blue said. She hated to disappoint Harley but he would have to live with disappointment in life like everybody else.

She had looked up his name in her dictionary. It meant "from the hare's or stag's meadow. (Anglo-Saxon)" Whatever a hare's or stag's meadow was, she mused.

She looked back at the *Victory.* When Harley arrived home from school they would finish the small jobs left. Everything, then, would be in readiness.

That night at the dinner table Mr. Colter proposed a toast from a bottle of red wine that stood by his plate. He poured a small glass apiece for the young people, a larger glass for himself and his wife. "A toast to the *Victory.*" He raised his glass. "And her crew."

Blue sipped at the wine. It tasted strange. The second sip tasted better.

Tibo, however, screwed up his face after one sip and left the drink unfinished. He made up for this with extra helpings of everything else. There was ice cream for dessert with beautiful, thick strawberry sauce and ground nuts, topped with a whirled gob of whipped cream.

Nothing would ever be like this again, Blueberry thought with a pang. At least not very soon.

The small bit of wine she had drunk made her feel sleepy. Tonight, of all nights, she must remain wakeful and alert.

Mr. and Mrs. Colter refilled their wine glasses, then led the way to the recreation room. There everyone relaxed, except Blue, chatting, discussing everything from the arriving tourists to the voyage tomorrow.

"No need to shove off at dawn," Mr. Colter said to Blue and Harley. "Take time for a hearty breakfast."

"I'm always hungriest at morning," Tibo declared.

Hunch was nearby in his cage. He had to go on the *Victory* with her and Tibo.

"Would it be all right," she asked the Colters, "if I take Hunch with me to the cabin tonight? It would make things go faster in the morning."

"Why, of course," Harley's mother said. "Harley, carry the cage over to the cabin when Linda and Tibo leave."

Soon after, saying she had various things to do, Blue said good night. Harley accompanied her and Tibo, carrying Hunch's cage.

"You get ready for bed," Blueberry ordered Tibo once they were in the cabin.

She stepped outside with Harley to take a last look

at Pinerest and the stars glimmering down through the tops of the pines and pale birch trees.

"I can hardly wait for morning," Harley said, sounding as eager as someone much younger. "I hope now you don't mind so much my going along with you."

"I don't mind." She looked at him. His hair seemed silver in the starlight. "But, well, I guess it's time to say good night." She held out her hand.

"Hey, it's not as if we're saying good-bye forever or something. See you in the morning."

She watched him walk away. Would he ever forgive her or understand, once he found out? She tried to imagine what it would be like if he were actually going with her: the surprise on the faces of people at Chicksaw Landing when Harley, handsome and trim, stepped from the *Victory*. In her second vision, she pictured his own astonished face when he saw the shack where she lived, Ma's nicotine-stained fingers, the gray dishrags, the flapping tar paper. No. It was far better this way, parting in the starlight, keeping something that would be beautiful always; for her, anyhow.

Back in the cabin, she looked at the electric clock on the vanity stand. Tibo sat on the edge of his bed in a pair of borrowed pajamas.

"You go to sleep," she said. "When I wake you, you do as I say without any questions or fuss."

"What d'you mean, Blue?"

"You'll find out. Though it's early yet, sleep fast."

She turned out the light and without removing her

clothes crawled into bed. She lay listening. A chirruping of frogs in a nearby slough. A distant car. Then, gradually, silence aside from the usual creakings and rustlings in the woods. Around midnight the yard lights would be turned off. Everything would have to wait until then.

The time seemed infinite until the lights, operated by an automatic timer, went off. Blueberry tiptoed to the cabin window. There was a haze of clouds over the moon but, even so, the landscape was brighter than she wished.

She shook Tibo. He woke with a small cry.

"We're leaving," she said. "Don't make any noise."

"But it ain't morning yet—is it?"

"No. We're going all by ourselves. Get your clothes on. Your old ones. We don't want to be accused of taking anything that's not ours."

Only half-awake, Tibo fumbled for his clothes and dragged them on. "They'll catch us, for sure, Blue. You're gonna get us into even more trouble."

"Stop worrying. I suppose you were so happy back at the Home! I suppose you had roast and gravy and ice cream there every day. Now, just hurry up and complain later."

Hunch was asleep, a cloth lent by Mrs. Colter fitted over his cage. With a prayer for his continued silence, Blue carried the cage, her knapsack riding her shoulders.

Together she and Tibo made their way to the shore.

The canoe glinted against the sand. "Wait here with Hunch," Blue whispered.

She stole toward the boathouse, pried a window open, slid the screen back, and hoisted herself over the sill. She reached for the canoe paddle, tripped and fell. An empty crate clanged to the floor.

Blue lay still, waiting. Only the frogs continued their throaty chants. Far off, a dog bayed. Otherwise, silence. She crept to the window and looked toward the Colter house. Darkness. The oar safely in her hand, she made her way back through the window to Tibo.

The canoe was marvelously light, she discovered. It took only a few minutes before she felt herself master of the paddle, feathering each stroke as Harley had done so as to make no noise. She would beach the canoe on the island where he would easily find it in the morning. Ahead now was the vague shape of the island. The *Victory* was lost in the shadows.

It was not until they were almost halfway across the long stretch of water between the mainland and the island that she permitted herself to look back toward the Colter house, hidden among sheltering trees.

Tibo gazed in the same direction. "I wish we could've stayed there forever," he said.

"Nothing is forever," Blueberry said.

The Landing

ON THE ISLAND, BLUEBERRY AND Tibo made a quick search of the deserted campsite to make certain that nothing of value remained.

"Why don't we light the lantern?" Tibo asked. "I can't hardly see nothin', it's so dark."

"We're not lighting anything until we're safely up river." She returned to the *Victory*, boarded it, and gave a final glance of inspection. Tibo followed.

"We're all set," she said, "except for one last thing I have to do. You wait here." In the cabin she drew out the box of wood carvings and in the dim light from the cabin window inspected the bluebird. It would have been perfect for Harley, but not with a broken wing. She picked up the figurine of a sleeping squirrel all curled around himself. It was extra special because she had carved it for Tad when she had still hoped he would come back. She made her way back to shore and to the canoe where she had pulled it up on the sand. She placed the carved squirrel on the stern seat where Harley could not miss seeing it.

"Ready?" she called to Tibo. She hoisted the *Victory*'s anchor, tossed the tow rope after it, then waded into the water. A few pushes and the boat rode free. She climbed back on board where she grasped the poling stick. "We don't dare start the motor until we're well out of sight and hearing."

He was gazing back toward the mainland. "I guess everybody's still sound asleep over there."

"The sounder the better." She thrust the long pole against the lake bottom, propelling the boat forward but staying close to the island's shore and shallow water.

"I bet they'll be mad when they find out, huh? D'you think they'll chase after us?"

"I don't know. Anyhow, we'll have a long head start."

Tibo breathed deeply of the night air. "It's kinda nice to be back on the *Victory* again, ain't it? Where're we headin' now, Blue?"

"I can't waste my breath talking. Poling this ship isn't like pushing a feather around." Hunch let out a loud squawk from the cabin and she saw that the cover had blown free from his cage. "Go cover up Hunch."

"Kin I have one of the cookies Mrs. Colter left?"

Blue shrugged. "I don't care. If you can find them." She saw him go unerringly through the cabin shadows to the cookie box. Here on the open water it was far lighter than under the shore trees.

When Tibo returned, munching, he studied her narrowly, his eyes glinting in a sudden ray of moonlight. "Maybe you won't tell me where we're headin' because you don't know, yourself. You said it was bad to end up just driftin'."

The words cut. "I'll tell you where we're *not* going, and that's Chicksaw Landing."

"But where else is there?"

Blue rested her arms a moment and visualized again a snug, window-shining cabin tucked back among pines. "We're going to Lena Finch's, that's where. We can be a big help to her and it'll be a place to stay out of sight until we can make new plans."

"She said she didn't want any kids around."

"That's because she was taken by surprise. It'll be different now when I tell her how we'll work hard for our board. And maybe I can carve more statues and sell them, saving up for the future."

Tibo nibbled a thumbnail, thoughtful. "I dunno. She could turn us right over to the cops or somebody, like the Colters done."

"They didn't do anything like that."

"Ends up the same."

"Not if we don't let it. I don't have time for chattering. Pretty soon now I'm going to start the outboard. Even if the Colters do hear it they won't know it's the *Victory.*" She did not need him throwing cold water on her plans. It was hard enough as it was to keep hope alive. If Lena Finch didn't want them around—well, she would have to think of something else.

"If they were gettin' a search party ready," Tibo said, "they must miss us some. Your ma was plenty worried, Mr. Colter said. Mr. Bert too, probably."

"If you're so eager to be back in Chicksaw you can hitchhike from Finch's Cove."

"I didn't say I wanted to go back there."

"Sounded like it."

He looked at her with a flash of defiance. "I just think your idea is dumb, that's all!"

She kept silent, shipped the poling stick, and went to the stern to start the *Victory*'s engine.

A few lavender-pink clouds floated around the sunrise. The wind was behind the *Victory*, giving it extra momentum as the craft throbbed upstream. Tibo sat at the tiller while Blue prepared a lavish breakfast: bacon, eggs, orange juice, and fresh bread.

"You can come eat first," she called to Tibo, "while I spell you at the tiller." She stretched, inhaling the aromas of food and the clean, morning-sweet air. "This is living!"

"Yeah! Everything looks brighter in the morning.

Maybe your idea wasn't so dumb after all, Blue."

"Everything's going to work out fine, one way or another," she said. "Here, your plate's ready."

She took her place in the stern. Now that they were back on the Little Skunk River she watched the shoreline for a chance sight of Smith. Perhaps he had gone back to Lena Finch's place himself. That would make everything perfect! She hummed a little. If it was off-key she didn't care; nobody could hear her above the chugging engine.

Following breakfast, they continued to take turns steering the boat. Shortly before noon, Blue was in the cabin, making notes in the log book, when Tibo yelled.

"Somebody's comin' fast right behind us. It looks like—it's the Colters' red speedboat!"

Blueberry stared. There was no mistaking the pilot. She joined Tibo quickly and took over the tiller.

"He's gainin' on us. Can't we go no faster?"

"We're already at full throttle."

A few minutes more and Harley was alongside. "You could have told me what you planned to do!" he shouted. "I wouldn't have stopped you. Put your darn motor on idle, will you?"

She cut the *Victory*'s motor entirely, and Harley set his to little more than a purr. His accusing, hurt look unnerved her as she faced him again. "I—I figured you'd feel duty bound to tell your folks," she said. "I didn't want you to have to lie for my sake."

"That's not the reason at all. You simply didn't want

me on board. Maybe you thought I'd give you smallpox or wreck the boat or something!"

She felt amazed. He had seemed so self-confident, even conceited, and now he seemed suddenly uncertain, imagining that she had run out on him because she didn't trust him or his skill.

"I know you could handle any kind of a boat," she protested. "I'm sorry about having to take your canoe—did you find it all right?"

He nodded. "I went over to the island first, to make certain the *Victory* was gone. I got up a lot earlier than usual—couldn't sleep. Right away I saw that the canoe was missing. Then I checked your cabin, woke my folks, and ran over to the island on the speedboat. The sun wasn't even up yet. Well, so here I am."

"Did you find the squirrel too?"

"Yeah," he said. "It's pretty neat."

He sounded sincere but she could tell he was still upset. "I left it to try to show you—that, well, I liked you. The reason I had to sail off by myself was because. . . . Simply because." There was no way to tell him about the shack at the Landing, or what her folks were like. "I mean it wasn't because of anything you said or did. You've been real nice and I. . . ." Her cheeks flushed. "Why'd you come after us? To take us back?"

"I guess that's the idea," he admitted. "I told my parents I'd try to catch up with you but I wasn't sure I could. I can just tell them. . . ." He considered. "I can say I saw you and that you were safely headed home so they won't worry and call out the river patrol or sheriff. You are heading home, aren't you?"

"Where else?" She avoided the clear blue eyes.

"And everything's okay with the *Victory?*"

"Shipshape. You and your folks don't have to worry about us, Harley. And thanks, heaps, for everything."

"You're welcome," he said formally. "Good luck." He added, "See you again sometime?"

"Maybe, sometime," she said.

The red boat circled away, picking up speed at the end of its turn. She watched until it was out of sight.

"He must have really gone at top speed," Tibo said, "to catch up with us this soon." He looked at her. "Are you in love with Harley?"

"In love!" she snorted. "I don't believe in stuff like that. And neither does he. We're just friends. That's the best."

"Like us, huh?"

The look in his dark eyes made her reply, "Right." Abruptly she started toward the galley. "I'll tidy up a few things while you pilot the ship."

By late afternoon, Finch's Cove was within sight. As before, there was no sign of life, no house visible. And no waiting Smith. Blueberry piloted the boat inward, cut the engine, then drifted to shore. There she cast the mooring line overboard, scrambled onto land, and snugged the line around a tree.

"Lower the gangplank," she called to Tibo.

He did and joined her on the strip of sand.

"Okay," she said, scanning the area. "Here's a kind of trail. It must lead to her house."

They followed the narrow path that zigzagged back and forth. Regularly, Blue stopped to whistle.

"You whistlin' for Smith?" Tibo asked.

"Not for that yappy terrier, that's for sure." She stopped. There, around a twist in the path, a house stood. "Come on!" She ran forward, then stopped still.

A rag of loose tarpaper fluttered from one corner of a small, sagging cabin. Above a moss-gnawed roof stood a rusty stovepipe. At one side of a parched yard was a small garden with a few pale lettuce leaves and some spindly green onions and corn. A rickety woodshed held a pile of corncobs.

And there, from beyond the shed, came Lena Finch. She held a .22 rifle in one hand, a dead pheasant in the other. The terrier trotted at her heels.

The dog stopped, stared toward Blue and Tibo, and barked. Lena Finch strode toward them, her coveralls flapping around her long legs.

"Well!" she exclaimed, confronting them. "What are you doing back here?" She seemed suddenly flustered and laid the dead pheasant cock on a bed of fern. "Spot here caught this bird and mangled it before I could stop him. So I had to shoot it."

"That's too bad," Blue said weakly, knowing it was illegal to kill a pheasant, cock or hen, out of hunting season. She wondered if the woman's story was even true.

"It'll make good eating, anyhow," the woman said.

"Spot caught himself a squirrel the other day, too. Squirrel pie is savory but roast pheasant is better."

"Yes, ma'am." Blue looked toward the shabby house again, the skinny yard. It was as bad as her own place unless the shining copper pots and pans were there inside. But Blue knew they would not be.

"I thought you were sailing off to see your uncle," the woman said. "You're back mighty soon. I found the carved chipmunk figurine, by the way. Nice work for your age."

"Thank you," Blue said absently, her gaze wandering to the battered house again. It could be fixed up some, with hard work. "Uh—we had to come back sooner than we planned. What I've been thinking is—maybe we could stay here awhile and, you know, help out. I'm kind of handy."

"I'm good at gardening," Tibo put in, following Blue's lead. "Back at the. . . ."

The expression on Lena Finch's face stopped him. She studied the pair, looking sad, and shook her head. "The place for you two, my dears, is back home where you came from. Now, all I have to offer before you leave is a piece of squirrel pie left over."

With a sudden show of pride, Tibo boasted, "We got lots to eat. Bacon and eggs and ham and. . . ."

Blueberry interrupted, "We could spare you a slice of baked ham, Miss Finch. And there's some chocolate cake."

"Heavens, I couldn't eat a thing right now!" Lena Finch declared although Blue noticed how her nostrils flared at the mention of the bacon, as if she could smell it frying. "Thank you, just the same."

There was only one thing left to hope for. Blue cleared her throat. "Have you happened to see a big gray cat with stripes and a white bib?"

"Any cats that come around here, I shoo off. Because of the song birds. The only cat I've seen was a small black one."

The terrier sniffed at the dead pheasant. A non-singing bird, Blue thought dully. "I guess it's so long then. We have to be shoving off." She began walking away.

"*Bon voyage*," Miss Finch called.

"What's that mean?" Tibo asked when they were beyond being heard. "Some kind of foreign language, wasn't it?"

"French, I think. It means have a good journey; something like that."

"A journey where, now?"

Blueberry kicked at a pebble on the path. "I have to think. What we'll do is go up river and anchor for the night. We can cook on board; Jed filled the kerosene tank."

"That Miss Finch looked awful poor. How come she turned down that offer of ham and stuff?"

"Pride. That's something a person can't ever afford to lose, no matter how poor they are."

"You can't eat pride. It sure wouldn't taste like much."

"No, but they say a person has to swallow their

pride sometimes. His or her pride, I mean."

Tibo studied the path. "Like if we had to go back to Chicksaw Landing?"

"Like that. But now let's get out of here. We can talk and think later."

"I'd sure have lots to tell the other kids if we did go back! A lot of 'em haven't been anywheres or even seen a big city. I bet Kelley's eyes will bug out when I tell him about that tall tower, and the bus, and all. And about that ice cream and all the other things we et at the Colter place! Man, the kids won't hardly believe it. Sometimes I think it was all a dream, myself, now that it's over."

Over. A dream. She stripped a leaf off a bush and kneaded it between forefinger and thumb. The words she had preached to Tibo drummed in her mind: You have to learn that dashing off without thinking where you're going is foolish. . . . But she *had* known where she was going. Hadn't she?

A bluejay called out hoarsely and the slight wind in the scrub pines was a whisper. The birds' voices, the wind singing to itself, gave no answer to her question. It seemed there should be a voice inside somewhere.

Go back home, Lena Finch had said. There had to be more to the journey than that because then nothing would have changed. Except within herself, she realized. Ma and Pa wouldn't change much, nor the people in Chicksaw Landing. The deep-down change had to be in her: Blueberry Lincoln Flynn. It had already started. She couldn't put it all into words yet but she could feel the words beginning to take form. When she had them just right, she would try to share them with Tibo.

He stood a bit away, apart, studying the ground as if he were trying to figure out some kind of answer too.

"I was just thinking, Tibo," she said as they began walking toward the boat. "In a way, you're closer to being nine now than to six. I mean, you've grown a lot."

He drew himself up. "I bet I've already grown an inch taller."

She hadn't meant it that way but she let it go.

Back in the *Victory*, Blue watched Finch's Cove fade from view while she steered the boat slowly forward. Hunch rustled around in his cage. Tibo sat with his back against the cabin wall, tying different kinds of knots with an old piece of rope.

"What happened to our harmonica?" he asked.

His tone nettled her, destroying the warmth she had felt toward him back at the Cove. Just because she had said he'd grown he threatened to get too big for his boots. "Since when was it *our* harmonica. It's safe in the knapsack—unless you sneaked it out."

"I never touched it! I'm not no thief."

"That's a double negative again. I told you about that before. I guess you'll never learn."

"What difference does it make?"

"Well, when you talk the way you do it shows you're ignorant and keeps you from getting ahead in life."

He fussed over a knot that would not come untied. "Some people are born smart, I guess. Like you."

"Are you being sarcastic?"

He looked at her, surprised. "No. I meant it, Blue."

She studied the river, then her fraying sneakers. "I'm not smart at all, Tibo. I'm as dumb as can be. And I'm a liar. But you know who I lied to most of all? Myself."

He was silent, then stood up, frowning. "Damn rope's all in a tangle. I'm gonna go and give Hunch a cookie."

She did not protest. Her eyelids felt heavy. The few snatches of sleep she and Tibo had had were not enough. Tomorrow morning, after a peaceful anchorage on the river, she would be able to face the decision that had to be made.

But when the time came for sleep, the *Victory* anchored in a small cove, the water lapping around the sides, she sat staring out at the star-gemmed river, sleepless. Tibo, too, crouched wide-eyed in the stern beside her.

"I'm gonna miss this old boat," he said.

"What d'you mean?"

"I mean, we're headin' back home, ain't we? There isn't any other place to go to now. Is there?"

She took a deep breath, then let it out, the words

forming slowly. "It's the only place to go before starting over again. Only, the next time I leave, I'm going to be truly ready." The answer had seemed to begin to take shape back in Finch's Cove but it had been there ever since she learned of Uncle Stewart's death. She hadn't been ready to face it then. "I'm going to study hard and get my high school diploma, and try to earn and save some money, somehow. I've been remembering something Abe Lincoln said." She looked up at the sky. The Big Dipper blazed there, brighter than a blue neon sign. "He said, 'I will study and prepare myself, and some day my chance will come.' "

"You gonna sail the *Victory* again?" Tibo's voice was eager.

"No." It was the hardest of all to say. "Except for short trips. But I'm going to repaint its name and put a flag on it. You can come along on those short jaunts. Or maybe you won't want to, since I let you down."

"You didn't let me down. But when you leave for good the next time, kin I go along?"

Again she groped for an answer, thinking of Tad. "I'm a lot older, Tibo," she said at last, "even though you've grown up—inside." She paused. "People have to make their own personal journeys separately, in their own way. You'll make yours someday. Until then we can help each other get ready. Okay?"

He studied the star reflections in the water. "I'd rather we could go together, like this time."

"It would be nice," she said. "This was a good trip in spite of everything. Lucky we weren't killed, though, there in the storm. You really came through, Tibo, when it counted. The thing is, in the future—you'll find your own way. That's the best thing to plan for."

He brooded, thoughtful, then turned toward her, his face brightening. "Yeah. But we'll be sharin' our plans together, in secret. So it's not as if we'd really be separate."

"That's sort of what I meant," she said, her voice soft. Tibo had somehow found the right words for both of them.

The day was clear, cloudless, with all the birds in Chicksaw County seeming to sing at once. Blueberry, at the helm while Tibo took his turn doing the dishes, watched the increasingly familiar landscape slide by. In spite of the singing birds and the splashes of sunlight among the trees, the woods seemed gloomy, empty. To fill that emptiness, she reflected, she would just have to adopt one of Smith's numerous offspring, if she could make certain which of the many kittens around was actually his.

She would have to try to look the other way when Pa was doing his spitting. It wouldn't hurt to clean up and try to decorate her own room a little, either. And maybe Ma would help her make a proper flag for the *Victory;* Ma was good at sewing when she wanted to be.

Hunch hollered from the cabin, "I want a cigar, dammit!"

Tibo came out of the cabin and pointed. "I kin see Chicksaw Landing comin' into sight. It ain't changed a bit."

"You sound as if we'd sailed around the world."

"Feels like it, almost. Hey, there's Old Sludge still sittin' on a rock, sunnin' himself."

Blue reduced the boat's speed. "Take the tiller a minute, captain."

Tibo blinked. "You didn't ever call me that before. I know it's only pretend but maybe—well, some day."

She went to the cabin, removed the harmonica from the knapsack, and returned.

She held out the harmonica. "You already know how to play it really well, and I never will."

He reached out, almost timidly, then cradled the instrument in his palm. "Jeeze—I mean, wow—you really want me to have it, Blue?"

"Sure. I think Tad would too."

"Wow," he said again, softly. "Will you come over to the Home and listen to me play sometimes? They might even let me be on some of the programs."

She shrugged, teasing, then smiled. "All right, if you learn to play even better." She turned. "We're here, mate."

Together they watched as the familiar shore came nearer, the stunted pines, the water striders skating against the current.

"Get ready for landing," Blueberry said.

"Aye, aye, sir!" Tibo moved to the prow.

Blue stood motionless, staring. Something moved

through the tree shadows, something on four, striped legs, with a white bib and a tall tail as straight as a flagpole.

"Well, I'll be. . . ." Blue murmured and then yelled, "Why, you blasted, faithless, no-good flea bag! You just wait—I'm going to give you the thrashing of your life!"

The *Victory* scraped sand, slid to a stop, and Blue leaped to shore. Smith sat licking a furry paw as if nothing had happened at all.

"First," she said, scooping him up into her arms, "I'm going to hug you to death."

Dry pine needles crackled. Blueberry looked.

"So you got home here finally where you belong."

Ma stood there. Voiceless, Blue nodded.

"That was a mighty long camping trip," Ma said. "I'm going to go and speak my mind to them teachers. Come here."

Holding her breath, still clutching Smith, Blue moved to her.

"We was getting worried," Ma said.

Tibo lagged a few steps behind Blue. He moved forward and touched her elbow. "Well, I'll see ya, Blue."

Blueberry turned. "Soon. And don't forget what we talked about last night."

His dark eyes glowed into hers. "I won't!" he vowed and trotted off in the direction of the Home, the harmonica clutched in one small, brown hand.